CROOKED CASTLE

A Twisty Thriller from the Casey Grimes Fantasy Universe

AJ VANDERHORST

The Casey Grimes Universe
stories in order...so far

CG#1
CG#2
CG#2.5
CG#3
CG#3.5
read anytime after CG#1
side stories

www.ajvanderhorst.com

Crooked Castle (A Twisty Thriller from the Casey Grimes Fantasy Universe)/AJ Vanderhorst. - 1st ed.

PRAISE FOR AJ VANDERHORST

★ 2020 Wishing Shelf Book Awards Silver
★ 2020 Readers' Favorite International Awards Contest
Bronze

"A steppingstone path of small mysteries and action scenes. Sylvan Woods is a splendid conception...fast moving and exuberant, packed with imagination." – *Kirkus Reviews*

"The Mostly Invisible Boy excels, venturing into unpredictable territory, combining the feel of a fantasy with a treasure hunt." – *Midwest Book Review*

"A true adventure, where the stakes are high, the danger real, and the goal is almost impossible to reach." – **Bookworm for Kids**

"The Mostly Invisible Boy is a gripping book from start to finish...riveting." – **LitPick**

"Brimming with intrigue, danger and humor." – **Book Craic**

"Original and inventive, full of courage and heart." – **Amy Wilson**, author of *A Far Away Magic, Shadows of Winterspell,* and *The Wild Way Home*

"Fun, funny and imaginative, The Mostly Invisible Boy is a rollicking good adventure." – **Andrew Chilton**, author of *The Goblin's Puzzle*

"Perfect for middle grade—not too scary but enough to keep you flipping the pages. Surprises at every turn keep the plot moving at a quick pace." – **Always in the Middle**

"Vanderhorst has created a character in Casey Grimes who is so relatable, and so tangible...a must-read fantasy novel for middle grade readers." – **Frank Morelli**, author of *No Sad Songs* and the *Please Return To* series

"A gripping fantasy adventure." – **Wishing Shelf Book Award**

"Incredibly imaginative and fun."– **Book Pipeline**

"Likable characters, clever plot, and unexpected twists and turns." – **Indie Reader**

"Vanderhorst connects to the deep feelings many middle school children deal with day in and day out." – **Reader's Favorite five-star review**

"Enchanting and unusual...the story entertains from the first page to the last." – **Story Sanctuary**

"A once-in-a-lifetime adventure. The characters are all so witty and eloquent, and yet the dialogue feels so natural and flowing. The story itself is fast-paced and fun, it doesn't ever get stuck on anything or leave you bored." – **The Artsy Reader**

"AJ Vanderhorst has the most beautiful imagination. The way he puts this world in your mind is nothing short of brilliant. The journey to Sylvan Woods had me on the edge of my seat, and I wouldn't have it any other way." – **Bookish Bliss**

"If you love unique and fun middle-grade fantasy stories with great and interesting characters, a cute little sister you can't help but love, a forest setting with a school and 'magical' community, lots of secrets and things just waiting to be revealed, monsters, missions and bravery... this is the book for you." – **Read to Ramble**

"Kind of gives off treetop Percy Jackson vibes, and I am totally here for it. I would love to get lost in the magical treetop world of Sylvan Woods, but I don't think I'd like to face all of those awful creatures! There's a lot of excitement and edge of the seat moments throughout the story, and the ending was no different." – **For Books' Sake**

"This is such a refreshing and delightful depiction of sibling relationships. In a world with magical trees, dangerous beasts, a far-off war and tree-top school for warriors there is such a rich font for the imagination. The over-arching idea of finding where you belong and fighting so that you can stay there is a great one." – **Broken Geek**

"This book had me on the edge of my seat." – **Reading Through the Looking Glass**

"An engaging and charming Middle Grade Fantasy story...and there's danger, too." – **I'm a Voracious Reader**

"The world with magic trees, vicious monsters, a far-off war that needs preparing for and a tree-top school for future warriors just speaks to my imagination and let it run wild." – **Tirilu**

"A bit Harry Potteresque...and what I hope will be a long series of adventures with Casey and his friends. But this is very much an original tale." – **The Strawberry Post**

Dedicated to people who are still looking for magic in hard places.

THE BOOKS...A QUICK INTRO

The Mostly Invisible Boy: Casey Grimes 1

Need friends? Try fighting monsters. Casey Grimes thinks his invisibility is permanent until he finds a secret forest society in charge of monster control.

Trickery School: Casey Grimes 2

Classes have begun. Please don't die. Monster-control academy starts for Casey & Gloria, but there's one little problem: A secret enemy who's playing for keeps.

Twisting Trails: Casey Grimes 3

Something's moving in the woods. Casey and Gloria finally have a chance to carve out a home in Sylvan Woods. But something is terribly wrong with the forest itself.

Dark Sky's Ashes: Casey Grimes 3.5

Let sleeping dragons lie. When Conley leaves his safety-obsessed neighborhood, he gets an ancient house with a secret that might roast him alive.

The Ghost of CreepCat (A Sylvan Woods Novella)

Track the ghost-cat! When Lila Banks takes a hike, she doesn't expect to be stalked by the ghost of her recently-deceased cat.

HOW 'BOUT?

Want a free Casey Grimes story?

Sign up for *The Sylvan Spy* at **b.link/Castle**

AIRDROP

OUCH, THE GIRL THOUGHT. *STOP SHOVING. LEAVE ME ALONE.*

She kept her eyes shut tight because she didn't want to wake up and get involved in a stupid fight. "No thanks," she mumbled. "Go away." You learned to sleep through a lot at the Orphan Foundation, but this was crazy.

Kids were yelling and crashing. Fluorescent flashes zapped her eyelids, someone being an idiot with the light switch. And someone had dumped a cup of water on her—or maybe they'd lost their minds and pulled the fire alarm, turning on the sprinklers? But the noise and the lights and the dripping didn't explain why she felt so uncomfortable, like someone had put gravel under her sheets.

Great, now I'm awake.

Her eyelashes brushed cloth, and she tossed her head, but the sheets stayed put like some genius had wrapped them around her face. *Ok, now I'm mad.* She rolled onto her back in the dark—*ow*—shrugged her cramped shoulders, and tried to push the stuffy cotton off her face, but she couldn't. Her hands were stuck behind her back. No, not stuck, tied. Someone had knotted her wrists in rope—and it wasn't loose.

A feeling like scorched wire twisted in her chest. *Ok, ooh-kay.*

She thrashed around, trying to get to her knees. Then a sharp gust of air caught her, not the Foundation's stale AC, and she fell sideways onto stone, not a bed at all. A flash of lightning lit up the ceiling, but in the sharp glare through her blindfold, she realized there *was* no ceiling—and rain was pinging off her skin, not fire sprinklers, and there were no sheets, just her damp clothes and the cloth across her eyes.

The metal in her chest got icy as the heat drained out of her.

"No," she whispered.

There was only one place she could be.

The Foundation's gravel roof was four stories high. On the ground, miles of asphalt took bites out of kids when they played ball or got knocked down. This wasn't a prank, not anymore. This was out of control. She got ready to kick and scream and fight the second someone touched her.

Then something swept past with an angry roar—something huge. Wind howled like it was being shoved out of the sky, and she wished her hands were free to cover her ears. Was it a helicopter? Had someone called the police?

"Right here!" she yelled. "Help me!"

Rock gnawed at her knees and elbows as she struggled upright. Lightning flashed, making her blindfold paper thin, and in a split second she saw—

empty sky

sharp rocks

big waves

She froze, swaying on her knees. *Weed, California, doesn't have a coast. No ocean, no wild wind. Where'd the Foundation go? Where's the helicopter?* She tried to catch her scampering thoughts: *Where's everyone else? How'd I get here? Why?*

Off to her right, someone screamed, the sound fading fast. Falling down and down.

Her teeth began to chatter. This was bad.

This was the kind of situation you got out of at any cost. The kind that could only get worse, like angry kids on a corner, shouting and pointing guns. You didn't stop to figure out why they were fighting. You just got out of there.

"God, where am I?" she said.

An explosion rocked her backward. The sky glowed red through her blindfold and what she saw got stuck in her retinas: a snaky, winged shape, fire blasting from its mouth. The girl's wet hair flipped in her face and rock bit into her palms as she twisted away. Cold flooded back over her as the bellows of the giant creature faded.

A flying, fire-breathing creature.

On a strange coast.

Hunting her. Hunting them.

Kneeling in the drizzle, she wanted to fall asleep. Black out and pretend she was somewhere else. *Someone* else. Now and then it worked, and you woke up in your bed, nervous and stiff, and the crisis was over.

In the Foundation, she'd sometimes slammed awake on the floor, seeing stars, when she'd been shoved out of her top bunk. Most of them didn't have railings, and some kids took advantage—the ones who had gangs and liked to roam at night. If she'd thought there was the smallest chance of waking up now, of escaping from the nightmare, she would've thrown herself over the edge, onto the Foundation's concrete floor.

But she knew it wouldn't work. This wasn't a dream, even though she'd been dropped on a rocky coast by a dragon. Even though there was no ocean in Weed, California, and no dragons, anywhere. This was real.

Waves crashed far below, a watery rumble.

"I need my hands," she whispered.

She rolled onto her back, tucked her knees, and stretched her wrists toward her heels, gritting her teeth. Stone scraped her spine as she rocked back and forth, and one of her hips throbbed angrily: *Ow–ow–ow.* In the next flash of lightning, she saw the tips of her old canvas sneakers, and she wrestled her hands across. *Halfway free.*

Wincing, she tugged off her blindfold. Wind tore the knotted cloth away, and she knew she was somewhere high, far from any city. She'd never seen a sky so dark, and she wondered where the other kids were on the cliffs—and who they were, whether they were from the Foundation or if they could be trusted.

Holding up her wrists, she found the rope in the starless night and bit, gnawing and spitting out fibers. She was a good biter—she'd always taken care of her teeth. The knots frayed after a few minutes and the wind snatched the cord away.

She tucked her head against the salty gusts. For a minute she held perfectly still, forcing herself to take deep, regular breaths the way she did when she was angry or so scared she could barely think.

Don't let the wind steal all the oxygen. Some of it's yours.

Sounds poked through the pitch black storm like needles: Rock clattering, the dragon's roar, screams. A haunted feeling crept over her, the feeling she got when a person was around, part of the scenery, and then, without warning, gone. An empty bunk, an empty desk, an empty corner. There were nights in the Children's Foundation dorm when you woke up, not sure why, and knew there were fewer kids than before. You wondered how long they'd been gone and what secret they'd known that let them get away.

She sensed the cliffs getting less and less crowded. Kids were trying to cheat the wind and rocks and waves—but they were failing. She shoved her hands against the stone so hard her arms began to shake.

Stay calm, she thought. Stay calm, and you can get out of this, maybe.

She pulled her knees to her chest to muffle her wild heartbeat.

Thunder rumbled. When the lightning lit up the hungry cliffs, she froze. Huge chasms looked like dirty, jagged shower drains. Slimy stuff dangled like moldy hair. She looked away and pressed a hand to her stomach. Her soaking sneakers were inches from the edge. She wanted to run and put her back against a wall, but there were no walls. Just spiky rocks and dark open space where the shore must be.

The lightning moved off over the ocean. For a second she saw towering waves, then darkness rushed back in. It started to rain, really rain, and she realized she couldn't wait this out. Her best chance would be in the morning, but if the wind got any stronger, it would snatch her and toss her like a sack of trash.

A sliver of moonlight found its way through the clouds, and the faint glow showed her towers of rock like broken glass. Nothing that looked like a path. No one else was moving—if there was anyone else left. Only someone crazy or on drugs would try to climb this.

But that's what she had to do.

She started crawling, scraping her bare knees, skinning her palms. She realized she was shaking and told herself it didn't matter. Not as long as she was moving forward.

"Think with your fingertips," she whispered.

The holds she found had sharp edges.

It's just blood, she thought. You've got plenty.

The worst moments were when she had to stand up and fling herself to the next ledge. The wind yanked on her arms. The left side of her body ached, pain radiating from her hip. The rain plastered her shorts and t-shirt to her skin. She knew the waves were watching and waiting, churning under the cliffs like the acid in your stomach that eats whatever falls in.

When she made the final jump, hair flying, hands outstretched and dripping reddish rain, she was sobbing. It's ok, she told herself. Ok to cry as long as you're still calling the shots.

Wet sand clung to her hands and knees and slid into her shoes but she didn't stop crawling. High grass whipped her face so she had to half-close her eyes. When the sun finally rose, she was a long way inland, inching her way through sand dunes—but the sound of surf kept pounding in her ear drums.

She'd made it. Wherever *it* was.

As far as she could tell, she was the only one.

THEY'D NEVER LET YOU GO

THE RAIN STOPPED, AND THE RISING SUN ADDED DULL BROWNS and greens to the wet, gritty world. Reaching the top of the latest sand dune felt like climbing a mountain, but another rose ahead. She sat down in a patch of thin grass, tucked her knees, and blinked sand out of her eyes. *Just a short rest.* Maybe she could get the grains out easier if she closed her eyes entirely...

When she woke up, the sun had ghosted to the far side of the sky. It wasn't diving out of sight, but it was getting heavy, glowing with watery orange haze that made long shadows on the dunes.

Without meaning to, she'd fast-forwarded the whole day. The darkening sand felt like a video game that had blipped and sent her back to level one where everything was dark and scary. Her torn fingertips ached when she pressed them to her forehead.

For a minute she felt confused. The dream she'd been having —about a gang of girls moving toward her in the Children's Foundation basement—felt more real than wherever she was. Then she took a deep breath and smelled salt and mud and sweat and blood. She dug her fingers into the sand, cupping broken sea shells.

It felt…sandy. Really sandy, like real sand.

That's right, I made it, she thought. The cliffs and the dragon aren't a nightmare, even though they should be. I was left here to die. But I didn't. I escaped.

She searched the sky for movement and saw nothing, aside from clouds like shredded gauze. When she moved, her head pounded. Scrapes on her arms and legs had started scabbing, dried blood mixed with sand. Lifting her shirt, she saw bruises where she'd thunked into rocks, and an ugly gash on her left hip, still oozing blood. She wasn't sure when it had happened—maybe when she'd made her first desperate plunge toward the shore. Her toes were bruised, her shoes ripped. Even her face had cuts that she didn't remember getting.

And the daylight was fading, turning the beach-like place into a vague, murky landscape. Not a normal beach at all. She hadn't been to one in years, not since she was little and fun and cute—but you didn't need recent memories to know that where there's a beach, there ought to be an ocean, blue and shimmering, lapping at the sand, filling in your footprints when you dance out of the way. But this ocean was a hungry gap at the end of a long, dark hole.

Her stomach shuddered.

You won't fall, can't fall now, she thought.

And then, because there was no one to hear her, she said it out loud.

"You're safe. You got away."

Her next thought was, Am I the only one?

She'd rarely been alone, as long as she could remember. Always fighting for space, fighting to hold a place in line, fighting to keep her bunk, fighting for grades, for safety, for attention. And usually failing.

Maybe someone else had made it and they'd missed each

other in the dark. Maybe that person was waking up on a different sand dune and having the same thoughts she was. Looking over her shoulder and thinking, If there's another person out there…do I really want to meet them?

"It depends…" she said out loud. Depended on who the other kid was. On whether she was a system kid too, on where she'd come from. What were the odds of meeting someone cool, not a thief or fighter or a liar, in a place like this?

Probably not great.

This seems like a horrible place, she thought, with kids from horrible places. Maybe my whole Foundation group got sent here. At the same time—look at all this room. All this sand, all these shells, all this sea grass. All this space.

The size of the beach washed over her. And she hadn't even stood up yet.

Finally she did, and walked slowly to the top of the dune to look back the way she'd come. Sand hills hugged the darkening sky in rolling, wet brown curves framed by sulky blue—still upset after the storm.

She could see her dented toe prints coming down then up, down then up, and the pointy scratches left by her fingers and the round imprints of her knees. There were wider drag marks where she'd flopped onto her stomach. Out beyond the dunes, the cliffs rose like broken project buildings full of violence.

There were no other prints in sight, and it made her feel totally alone.

She thought she should probably go back and look for survivors, but her gut slammed up at her heart like a closed fist, and she knew she couldn't. Just couldn't. At least not yet. If there were others, she'd have to find them later. Not that she had anything to offer.

Hi, it's me, a kid with zero assets just like you.

Could the rest of them really all be gone?

The dragon had dropped lots of them. At least a dozen, she was sure.

You learned to see a lot without sight, sleeping in shared dorms.

Her senses told her they were gone. Swept into the sea like rinds into a garbage disposal.

She swallowed and gave her shoulders a shake.

"You don't know for sure," she said. "Here's what you *do* know. Dragons exist. You're by the sea. No one cares if you die."

The first two bits were brand new pieces of information.

She wondered how long it had been since she'd stretched out in her top bunk, her toothbrush and a sharpened fork under her pillow. A day? Two days? A week? How much time had gone by since she'd woken up on the cliffs with the dragon roaring overhead?

She didn't feel older. She held up her hands and inspected her beat-up nails. They weren't especially long. So maybe it had just been a day or two. But that really didn't matter. What mattered was all this…

She looked inland, shading her eyes. Over the edge of the next dune, she caught a glimpse of waving, grassy fields, and in the distance something spiky and dark that might be trees. Maybe if she hiked far enough, she'd cross a protected wetland and stumble into a parking lot. People would stop walking their dogs to stare at her. "Sweetheart, are you ok? Here, take this blanket. Let's get you to a doctor." And she'd say, "Yes, please. And just so you know, there's a dragon out there, so stay close to your cars and keep your dogs on their leashes."

Once she made it back to civilization, she'd slip out of the doctor's office and down an echoey stairwell like people did in movies, and she'd hit the streets and keep her head down until she turned eighteen.

Eighteen. Hmm. She blinked and frowned. How long until

that happened? Five years? Four? She chewed her lip. Well, she'd remember later, when her mind unfogged itself.

But who would let you wander the California coast? They'd keep marking you down on their lists as long as they possibly could. They'd keep adding more pages to your file. When would they ever set you loose? When would they ever let you you go? She frowned and answered herself out loud.

"Never. Absolutely never."

That's when she knew—or almost knew—she was on an island. Even though she wanted to believe it wasn't true, and that she'd been dumped in a strange wildlife sanctuary by mistake. *A huge mistake involving a dragon. Yeah, that's believable.* She turned to look at the cliffs again. The black rocks caught the tired sun over the dunes and threw rays at her eyes like shards of glass.

"I'll make it work," she said. "I'm not going back to the Foundation, ever."

She turned back inland, thinking, How bad can island life be? People survive this kind of thing all the time, and some of them even—oh!

Her hand flew to her heart.

A boy stood waiting.

If her voice hadn't been raw from the saltwater and night air, she might've screamed, the absolute worst thing to do. Instead she groaned, a sound straight from her soul, and got ready to fight.

THE FOX

THE BOY LOOKED LIKE SOMEONE YOU DIDN'T WANT TO MESS WITH. He studied her with dark eyes, his weight rocked back on one leg, a hand on his hip. His faded jeans were patched but in good shape. His shirt was a dull gray, sleeves rolled to the elbow. He didn't swagger too close, didn't mouth off, didn't try to touch her hair.

He's in control, she thought. He's dangerous.

Maybe she wouldn't win but she wouldn't roll up in a ball either. The important thing was to show that no one told her what to do. She got her balance in the sand, tightened her fists until they were white, and narrowed her eyes to slits.

He nodded. "Hope I didn't startle you."

She didn't move.

"I get it," he said. "I'd keep my distance too, but congratulations on making it." He ran a hand through rust-colored hair. "We used to rush to the cliffs and throw ropes when we heard the dragon roaring, but then the blindfolds started happening, and when kids heard our voices, they tried to walk toward us like they—what's the word?—like they, um, counted on us one hundred percent."

"Trust?" she said. "They trusted you?"

"Yeah, that must be it." He trailed off. "Anyway, it's suicide to sleep out by the cliffs at night. We don't want to, but we have to let the new arrivals go it alone."

New arrivals, she thought. This has happened before.

"Did anyone else make it?" the boy asked.

She didn't see what she had to lose by telling the truth. If she lied, he'd figure it out.

"I don't think so," she said.

"Ah, that's too bad." He sighed and touched his chin.

She thought of everyone out there on the cliffs. Wherever they'd come from, whether she'd have recognized their faces, they were probably all ghosts now.

All except her.

The boy was studying her. He didn't seem hostile, but he didn't make her feel relaxed. His eyes were friendly but sharp. He was a capped needle, a knife in a drawer.

You've got to be careful, she thought. Until you figure out how to handle him.

"So what's your name?" he asked.

"My name is…" She blinked.

Where had it gone? She shoved the darkness and the cliffs away and thought, Your name, your name is…but nothing came. A white blur rushed behind her eyes—and a single, quavering scream. The scream was a blue-black wisp of shadow, twisting through the empty whiteness. It left her breathless and confused.

She saw the look on his face.

"It's gone, huh? The names usually are, so there are a lot of us running around with made up ones. Some kids even call themselves 'Cliff.' Little inside joke, just until they remember their real names, except they never do—or until they think of something better, if they get enough time. Want me to call you Cliff for now?"

"Not a chance." Her torn nails bit into her palms. Cliff was a horrible name for someone who'd survived the Cliffs. You might as well say, Hi, I'm Drowning. Hi, I'm Blood Loss. Hi, I'm the Children's Foundation. She tried to think of something better. Clean, safe, far from the sea.

"What's going on in there?" The boy said. "C'mon, talk to me."

She licked her lips, noticing how cracked they were. And salty. She needed water. Clear water, not the ocean. A creek, a stream.

"Brook," she said. "You can call me that."

The boy raised an eyebrow. "Nice to make your acquaintance, Brook. I'm very happy you're alive. I go by Fox." He rolled his eyes toward his scalp. "My hair, you know. The name just stuck." He extended his hand.

"Makes sense," she said.

After she made sure his palm was empty, she didn't hesitate. Hesitation implied a lack of confidence.

They shook.

"It's a good thing I ran into you," Fox said.

"Why's that?" Brook wished she sounded more confident, the way she would've at school or on the street, where she was quick to prove she didn't need help, especially when someone offered it.

Fox smiled. "Maybe you've noticed, this is kind of a scary place."

She crossed her arms because she didn't have an answer to that. She didn't want the island to be a scary place. And she didn't want to ask too many questions, because questions showed how little you knew. But sometimes you could find out what you wanted if you played an angle. Circled around. Like the way you could sneak through the kitchen and steal a chocolate milk if you said you needed to see the nurse. But you never asked to visit the kitchen.

"Have you seen the dragon?" she said, taking a risk.

Fox didn't act surprised by the question, which was good.

"More times than I'd like," he said. "There's no killing a thing like that. Did you get a good look?"

She shook her head no. "But it was right above me. Breathing fire."

"Usually I only see its fire," Fox said. "At night, miles away. If you ever see it flying toward you, start running. Hide in the woods if you can. Even then, it'll get you if it wants to. Once it locks onto a kid, there's almost no chance." He frowned. "The only safe place is the castle."

"Castle?" Brook said before she could stop herself.

You dummy, she thought. You had him talking.

"Yeah." He swept an arm inland. "Do you know the word?"

Brook pictured a towering building made of stone.

"Like in movies," she said.

"That's right," he said. "Like Lord of the Rings. High walls, huge gate. It's where you want to be on this island, believe me."

So why aren't we walking there? Brook wanted to say. And did we go back in time? What is this, medieval Europe? Instead, she asked: "Is that where you live?"

The boy frowned. "If only. The blue-faces own the castle, and those kids don't share. They'd rather cut your throat than let you in, like their paint makes them better than the rest of us. You won't find them out here, scrapping in the dirt and rain, fighting to survive."

His eyes gleamed.

Brook thought he might actually snarl.

Fox took a breath. "They've owned the place as long as I've been here. The castle is closed to survivors like us."

Like us. She appreciated that.

"What do you do then?" She didn't want to sound like she was prying, but luckily Fox seemed happy to have someone to talk to. Well, she could be a great listener.

"Me?" he said. "Oh, nothing special. I do my best to keep my distance from the killers. I help where I can, but I try to steer clear of trouble, which can be a challenge. Sometimes I just think about better days." Fox glanced at the sky. "Speaking of trouble, I need to be getting back."

"Ah, ok," Brook said, wondering what he meant by *killers*.

They'd been chatting in the shelter of the dune, and it had been such a relief to talk with someone normal that she hadn't noticed the shadows getting long. On the inland side of the island, the sun was sinking behind the trees in a gold pool, spraying the sky with swooshes of creamsicle and grape. She stole a look at Fox. He was rolling his shoulders, watching the sun go down as well.

"You probably have a plan," he said. "You seem on top of things."

"Thanks," she said. "I do my best."

But I don't know a thing, she wanted to add. I don't know where I am.

"I'll see you around, Brook." He gave her a half smile and started away, following his own prints back along the dunes.

SURVIVAL CHOICES

BROOK'S SHOULDERS TWITCHED AS SHE WATCHED THE BOY GO. SHE wanted to scream, *Wait! Let me come too*. She'd say, Our chances will be better together, against the dragon and the blue-faces and whatever.

But she couldn't say that. Because that's not what Fox would hear.

"Help, I'm trying to act tough, but if you shove me I'll crumble into pieces"—that's what he'd hear.

She couldn't stop her hands from shaking, so she put them behind her back. It's ok, she thought. As long as you're still in charge. She didn't say a word as Fox's shape got smaller.

Maybe she could dig a hole in the sand, just for tonight. Tomorrow she would figure something out. What did people do on desert islands? Eat berries, make fires with rocks, stay warm in caves? Maybe tomorrow she'd find some berries. Or she'd go looking for a cave. Yeah, that's what she'd do. Or maybe lightning would strike a dead tree and she'd grab a flaming branch and…who was she kidding?

Fox's shape looked about six inches tall in the distance. His legs were hidden by waist-high grass when he stopped moving and froze like a glitch in a video. A few seconds passed, then he turned and started back, a gray silhouette against the painted sky. Brook held her breath. What if he was taking a different trail? Maybe he'd walk all the way up to her, give her a nod and keep on going: "Sorry, Brook, I forgot something. Good luck."

Minutes went by.

Fox got closer. The backlight gave his head a coppery glow.

He stopped five feet away.

"No offense," he said. "But I realized maybe you hadn't had time to collect firewood or make plans to defend yourself. If you already have, just say so, I don't mean to be rude."

Brook took a quick breath through her nose. "I'm working on it," she said.

"Cool. Well." He nodded to the sunset. "You'd better move fast."

He started away again, but it was too much. Brook held out for five more seconds.

"Wait." At least she hadn't screamed.

When he turned, he looked curious but not surprised.

"If you don't mind, maybe I'll come too." It took all her self-control not to wince as the words left her mouth. She hadn't begged. But who was in charge now?

Fox didn't rub it in.

"That's great," he said. "I didn't want to be pushy. Everyone has to be careful out here, but you seem like one of the good ones. C'mon, we've got just enough time to get back before dark."

Brook fell into step beside him, looking away so her face could return to normal. Her skin tingled and she was pretty sure she'd gone pale.

"Is there any water?" She'd fallen this far, she might as well fall a little deeper into Fox's debt. Her mouth felt as dry as sand.

"Absolutely," he said. "And some food. I have enough to share."

"Cool, thanks," she said, and did her best to act all casual, so he wouldn't know she felt like crying—or cheering. Or maybe both.

They left the dunes and crunched through fields as the sun dropped lower. Salty breezes streamed past, tossing the high grass. Brook couldn't hear the waves anymore or see the sharp, dark cliffs, and that helped her relax. Now the turf had some bounce under her feet. The forest loomed closer, inky-green and thick. They pushed through leafy bushes and little trees.

"The key is to stay out of the way," Fox said. "Let the bad stuff flow right past you like a train you don't have to take. It's why I like the edges of the forest. You don't want to go too far in, at least not at night. Some kids would say the woods are never worth it, but I disagree. It's not good to be out in the open when the sun goes down. It's even risky during the day."

"Yeah," Brook said. "Makes total sense."

She was actually thinking, Why so risky?

"Now we're halfway to camp," Fox said.

"Is that like halfway home?" Brook said.

"Um—sure, I guess."

They pushed into the woods on a thin dirt trail. At first the trees kept their distance, but as she and Fox got deeper and the sun got lost behind black, twisty branches, the plants got grabby, sticking their twigs into the trail and waving prickers near Brook's ankles. She had to keep ducking and sidestepping —which made it even harder to focus.

What's my name? she kept thinking. Who am I, am I, am I? She wanted to smack the side of her head, like maybe she could jar it loose. Meanwhile, there were big gaps in what Fox was telling her. She was happy he seemed talkative. It meant she was learning a lot. The problem was, he assumed she was smarter than she was, or that she'd caught on more quickly than she had.

Fox must've been dropped on the cliffs like her, so at some point his brain must have been going crazy too. Darting from thing to thing. Struggling to keep up. But apparently he'd forgotten what it felt like to wake up on the rocks knowing absolutely nothing, because he was giving her too much respect.

Too much respect. Ha.

"Now we're in the middle woods," Fox said. "Not the edges and not the deep dark part, kind of walking a line between the two. Other kids don't come in here at night."

"Cool," Brook said. Wait, what? she almost added. *Why are we in here then?*—but caught herself. Because *respect*. Respect was something you never gave back once you got it. Like being handed a wad of cash. As soon as the paper brushed your palm, you put it somewhere safe and didn't flaunt it, didn't give it away without a fight.

But she hoped there was a good reason they were twisting their way through dark, prickly woods as the sun went down.

SNATCHED BY THE FOREST

"ACH!" BROOK WALKED THROUGH A SPIDERWEB AND SWALLOWED A gasp, then stuck out her bottom lip and blew, trying to float the stickiness off her face. When that didn't work, she half-closed her eyes and wiped her lashes. In the low light, she didn't see the spider. It had better not be riding in her hair.

"Watch out for spiderwebs," Fox said over his shoulder.

Brook wondered if he was grinning. "Thanks—I'll do that." She ran her tongue across her teeth and spit. She'd have to be more tuned in, like she was walking down an alley. But that was tough, the way her brain was buzzing.

Buzzing like a fly in a web, she thought. Ugh, that's gross.

She picked up a branch to hold in front of her face.

But she *was* stuck in a sticky place. If Fox had told her everything was going to be all right, or said, "Girl, you're too pretty to worry about details," she would've taken her chances by herself. She would've hit him and said, "Ok, what's up now?" Having his respect made things complicated. Questions she couldn't ask tumbled around her mind.

What do we drink?

What do we eat?

Who are we hiding from?

What happens at night?

Sure, there were other questions, like What is this place? and Why are we here? But those hardly even counted. Questions that big didn't get answered, never did. They didn't even get asked unless you were, hypothetically, talking with a friend.

Fox might be friendly, Brook thought, but he's hardly a friend. He seems like he knows what's going on, which is good, and maybe he's more trustworthy than most, but that's it. Take it for what it's worth. If I'm patient, things will start coming into focus and I'll figure out what's going on. So stay calm and play along.

"At least we get nice sunsets," she said, realizing she'd been quiet. When you were too quiet, people started giving you weird looks.

"We sure do." Fox paused to admire the sky. The trail was long gone, and they were shuffling through dead leaves and shoving their way through thick landscapes—thick forest-scapes, thickets?—whatever you called them, dodging the spiky fingers of the bigger trees.

"I sort of collect sunsets," Brook said so Fox would think she was the sharing type. "This one looks like rainbow sherbet with extra raspberry. I'd give it an seven point five out of ten."

"Seems about right," Fox said. "I should enjoy the sunsets more. Whatever happens, they're one thing no one can take away from you, right?"

Brook opened and closed her mouth. How did he know that? She remembered nights on the rusty fire escape, sitting by herself, when she'd thought the exact same thing. Hearing someone else say it out loud was crazy—and it made her think, Hey Fox, you're ok. But what she said was, "Hey Fox, you're kind of a philosopher."

He smiled over his shoulder.

She watched the colors melting into the spiky black nastiness of the forest, and thought, It *looks* like the same sky as Weed, CA—but you probably can't guess your location from a sunset. She thought of an ancient map she'd seen in one of her history books. The world looked flat like a magazine and if you sailed off the edges, the map said, Here be dragons. What if she and Fox had been dropped into some wild and forgotten corner of the world? Well, not a corner, more like a floating, abandoned lot.

Because there *was* a dragon.

She really, really wanted to ask:

Hey Fox, do you have any theories about, you know, all this?

Since you've got a philosophic streak and all?

Instead, she slashed at a spiderweb and took three deep, slow breaths to clear her mind. Then she hiked a little faster to catch up with Fox. The trees were bigger and more bristly now, stealing all her personal space. If these trees were human they'd be picking a fight. Browns and greens were fading to gray, and the ground felt rough and cluttered. Brook stole glances right and left as she scuffed over roots and rotting wood, trying not to twist an ankle. Hooky branches kept snatching at her clothes. Keeping track of all the prickly, sticky threats was a full-time job.

These woods are not the nice kind, she thought.

It made her forget to keep chatting up Fox.

"Doing ok back there?" he said.

"Oh, doing great," she said. "The spiders aren't winning!"

He glanced back, but the darkness had swallowed his face, like he was a villain who'd turned away—*surprise*—and pulled on a mask of shadow.

Brook flinched. If Fox *had been* a villain and *had* tried to scare her—and she knew he wasn't but if he *had* been—well, then it worked. She stopped walking. No one can see you, she thought. No one can hear you. You're not even carrying a sharpened fork. She let the space between them grow to a safer distance and pretended to pull leaves out of her hair. The open ground behind her had been eaten by trees and shadows. Fox said this was the middle forest, but it seemed deep and dark to her.

You're lost, she thought. Lost on a lost island. Of course you are.

If she turned and walked in a straight line, maybe she could get back to the fields, but she wouldn't bet on it. If she ran, she'd never find her way out. The sun was disappearing behind black, grabby branches and there weren't any obvious ways to escape. No wonder other kids didn't come here.

She wasn't sure she wanted to be close to Fox in the dark—especially when she couldn't see his face. Thinking about her options—turn and walk away; stop and hide; or keep following Fox—she took her eyes off the woods. A second later, she felt herself pulled up short. Her chin jerked to one side, her heart punched her chest, and her hands flew up to fight—but Fox was still in front of her, walking away. He hadn't touched her. When she turned her head, she saw a thorny vine twisted in her long, tawny hair. The forest had snatched her. Snuck in while she was spacing and said, *Gotcha*.

She took a handful of hair and yanked.

"Oww." Now the thorns were stuck deeper.

"Tangled up?" Fox appeared beside her. "Hey, you're only making it worse."

Brook tried to think of something to say as the woods and the night closed in like walls. "I got my name wrong, didn't I?" she gasped. "Rapunzel—that's what I should've called myself." She forced a smile.

"Here, let me," Fox said.

A sharp edge gleamed in his hand.

Brook froze. If she'd been at school or at the Foundation, she would've turned to run. But the forest was holding her down like bullies by the lockers.

Fox's knife shone in the dark like a razor.

HIDDEN FIRE

BROOK JERKED AWAY BUT HER HAIR SNAPPED HER BACK.

"Easy, Fox, easy." She held one hand in front of her chest and forced herself to keep talking. "Um, is that a knife? Cool, I'll bet it comes in handy." Her heartbeat drowned her words—THUMP, THUMP, THUMP—like music in a club, so loud you could hear it from the street. She tugged at her hair with her free hand, but she might as well have been tied down. She couldn't have trapped herself better if she'd tried.

"Seriously," Fox said.

THUMP.

"Stop moving," he said.

THUMP THUMP.

"That's not helping, Brook."

She let go of her hair and held up her palms like they were force shields that would blast Fox backward like Ironman. Of course, that wasn't how it worked when a blade met your skin. She curled her fingers into fists, then forced them to her sides and tried to put some laugh into her voice.

"Hey Fox, can I borrow that knife?"

"How much do you care about your hair?" Fox said at the same time.

Then *he* laughed and she joined in a second later, trying not to sound crazy.

"Seriously, though," Fox said. "Do you want me to chop the vine or your hair?" He glanced around the darkening woods, shadows pooling under trees like the night was about to flood upward from the ground. Wind whistled overhead. They could have been in a dead end alley or an empty basement.

Brook noticed he didn't offer her the knife.

"Um, cut the vine," she said. The further the blade stayed from her skin the better. She forced herself to hold still as Fox moved close. His arm brushed her elbow. She smelled the metal very near her face and held her breath because she wanted to grab for the knife or lash out with her elbows or knees—but it wouldn't work. She'd end up with sliced fingers and she'd still be trapped, and then Fox would pick himself up, brushing off dirt—and he'd be mad.

Please let him be a good person, she thought. Please please please.

With a crunch, the bramble released her.

"Thank you," Brook breathed.

"It's kind of a mess," Fox said, "but you can figure it out later. Let's go."

A wave of shuddery tension flowed out of her. She smoothed her hair against her shoulders and would've tucked it inside the collar of her t-shirt, but Fox was right. The vine had made a tangled knot, and she didn't want the thorns stabbing her back.

Thank God, she thought, Fox isn't a bad person.

Her feet felt lighter in her dirty shoes as she followed him through the shadows. A few minutes later, heavy shapes rose around them like an underpass, making the dark complete. Brook followed the sound of Fox's steps with her hands spread out, feeling the way. Her fingers brushed rough stone on either side as they moved down a narrow, maze-like path. Then she smelled woodsmoke, they turned a corner between two standing stones, and the darkness lifted. Reddish light glowed on smooth rock walls. They stood in a sunken hollow facing the glowing embers of a small campfire.

Brook felt like a door had swung shut on the darkness.

"Finally," Fox said. "That was pushing it, but we're safe now. Welcome to the best campsite on the island—not counting the castle, obviously." He smiled at her. "No one can sneak up on us. And nothing will see our fire either. This is as good as it gets."

"It's perfect," Brook said. Upright boulders disappeared into the blue-black night. When she looked up, the sky was mostly hidden by the branches of greedy trees. She would've liked to see more stars. But it was good the trees were there in case the dragon flew by.

A sound drew her to the far side of the hollow. At first she couldn't believe her ears, but sure enough, water trickled down a grooved boulder, splashing into a mossy pool. Maybe the campsite really was perfect.

Fox must have seen the longing on her face. "Go ahead," he said.

Brook threw herself down, cupped her hands, and gulped the cool, clear water. The drink was the best news she'd had since she'd woke up on the cliffs. Good news, the water said as it washed the salt off her lips, off her teeth, off her tongue. There's hope. Maybe, just maybe, something good will happen.

She sat up, wiping her face. "How long have you been here?"

"On the island, you mean?" Fox had added twigs to the embers and was prodding them with some kind of metal poker. "Or here?"

"Both." Brook smiled.

"Well…" He laid a stick on the coals. "I kept track of days at first. Then I kind of stopped counting, because it wasn't helping me. Just making me a little crazy." He touched his forehead. "You know what I mean?"

"Do I ever." She'd long ago stopped counting days at the Foundation.

"It was at least a couple months," Fox said. "I walked around the edges of the island, scoping things out. I hid from the dragon, met some other kids, and tried to get into the castle, but that went badly. Then I lost track until I found this place. After that, I started counting again. I've been here, let's see, eighteen days now. It's special."

"So you haven't been here years?" Brook said. "That's a relief."

He laughed. "Years, ha! Definitely not. But a few months, probably. I haven't seen a boat or a plane or anything. No one else comes here, no one but the dragon. You'll want to look for yourself, but you can't see land from any of the beaches."

Brook pushed the chunk of bramble off the back of her neck. It was pricking her skin like tiny claws. She wondered whether to risk another question.

"What do you think you'll do about your hair?" Fox asked.

The thorns were twisted in her locks like a little hair-destroying machine. There was only one choice, but it didn't make her happy.

"I think *I'll* have to cut it," she said, choosing her words. Fox could have killed her or hurt her in the forest and he hadn't, but she still didn't want him cutting her hair.

"Probably smart," Fox said. "The island is a prickly place."

"Understatement," she said, wondering if he was playing it cool on purpose.

"Here," Fox said.

Brook perked up, thinking he was about to hand her the knife, but instead he held out some dried meat. "Hey, thanks." The meat didn't smell bad, just smoky. Delicious, if she was being honest. She bit off a piece, her mouth swimming, and forced herself to chew it until it got soft, which meant about twenty times.

"Rabbit jerky," Fox said proudly. "Lots of them around. Of course I could kill something bigger, but rabbits, well, you don't waste anything, and they don't have fangs or talons or stingers to pull out, and they actually taste good."

"So good," Brook said. And she meant it. She found it hard to concentrate on much else as she tore at the jerky with her teeth, eating a shred at a time. Fox put two more sticks on the fire. The flames threw flickering lemon-gold light on the rock walls, making the camp seem warm and safe. And it *was* warm by the small fire, out of the wind. And if Fox was right, it was safe too. Safe from the sea, the cliffs, the dragon, and whatever else was out there.

FIVE CAREFUL CUTS

"You can have more rabbit if you want," Fox said. "I wouldn't recommend it, though. When you haven't eaten for awhile, it's smart to go easy on your stomach."

"Makes total sense," Brook said. The first hunk of jerky had mostly filled her up, but it was a nice gesture. Fox didn't have to give her food. Or let her drink his water. Or share his secret campsite. She didn't want to push it. He sat cross-legged in the dancing light of the fire, shoving it with the poker like he was trying to get the flames just right.

Now that Brook was no longer starving or dying of thirst, another sharp, twisty urge was rising in her chest. It wasn't a weird question about the meaning of life. It was an obvious one. She was getting the words ready when Fox held out his knife. She was so surprised her hand flew halfway to her mouth.

"Here you go," he said. "Hard to sleep with thorns in your hair."

She'd been wondering how the little drama would play out. Maybe she'd have to point out that her hair wasn't going to cut itself. Or ask if he had a pair of scissors lying around. She would've done both those things before she asked point blank to borrow his knife. Worse than asking a random kid for his address. Luckily it hadn't come to that.

She leaned forward on an elbow and reached, wondering if Fox would snatch the knife back at the last second. Instead she had the feeling, as she lifted it off his palm, that he'd put the moment off as long as he possibly could, and was forcing himself to let go. The knife felt heavy with Fox's mind hanging on to it. He kept his dark eyes pinned to her as she slid away to the far side of the fire.

Brook felt like a dog with a bone. For a split-second she could've jumped to her feet and sprinted into the night—but of course she'd just get lost. Instead, she touched her hair and sighed, and she wasn't faking. As she ran her fingers up her neck, she wished her hair had been twisted in a topknot, or pulled back in a ponytail or even braided.

Yeah, if only you could've been dropped on the cliffs with your hair done.

"This isn't going to be pretty," she said.

She'd never admitted it, but now she saw those Foundation kids were right, at least a little. Always on her case: "What's up, Shampoo Princess? When you gonna open your own salon?" She'd done her best to hide it, but she'd been proud of her hair, the whispery weight, the ways she could make it look good. Now she had to hack it off.

When she looked up, Fox was still watching.

"Wanna buy a ticket?" The words shot right out.

His eyebrows jumped and he looked into the fire.

"I mean, no big deal..." Maybe she'd been a little harsh.

"No, I get it." He kept his eyes on the blaze. "A haircut is personal."

Not to mention, Brook thought, this is a very sharp knife. She ran her thumb along the edge, glad he'd stopped staring so she could focus.

Then she swallowed and grabbed a handful. Dusky brown

with amber streaks from the sun, now it smelled like the ocean. Pulling the hank away from her head, she raised the knife and sliced in a careful arc. At first she thought nothing had happened. Then the bramble bumped her wrist, dangling from the tangled mess in her hand. The knife was *really* sharp. It made her think of the hours she'd spent in her dorm, grinding away at her fork to give it razor edges. Her *shork*, she'd called it. Not a spork. Not a fork. A sharp-fork or even a *shark*-fork. A shork.

One of her better jokes, even though she'd kept it to herself.

She wanted to end the haircut right there, with the thorns sliced away, but she could imagine what she looked like and it would take a lot of product—and some dye and face piercings— to make it look like she'd done it on purpose.

Brook sighed and found another handful. The knife moved through it soundlessly. No sawing needed. Two more cuts and cool air swept the top of her spine. I wonder what I look like now, she thought, and frowned. *Short hair, don't care.*

She swept her left hand back and forth, collecting strands, and finished the job with a delicate swoop of the blade. She ran her thumb along her naked neck, feeling feathered edges. Her fingers found the hollow at the bottom of her skull, the place where your spine connects to your brain, a place you always keep safe. Now open to the air.

She shivered.

I look like a prank, she thought. She almost wished Fox had been watching, because seeing her now, changed all at once, it would hit him like a bad joke.

"Hey, what happened?" he'd say. "Where's that girl who was sitting there?"

She didn't like being laughed at. It made her tense inside. Then something slipped away from her like a breath of air. Her shoulders sagged. It doesn't really matter, she thought. Of course it doesn't. *There are no mirrors here, no combs or headbands.*

Still, it was hard to let go of how she looked. To lose a part of herself to the island.

Maybe Fox sensed her lack of movement, because when she looked up, he was watching.

"Hey, you did a great job," he said. "You look good."

"Thanks," she said grudgingly. Was he lying? On this island, she'd never know. She stepped around the fire and gave him back the knife and he nodded up at her.

"Yeah, it's nice."

"Don't push it," she said, wishing she had a knife of her own.

He held up his hands in fake surrender. *Ok, ok.*

So she gave him a smile as she sat back down on the far side of the flames. And then, because they seemed to be getting along, she asked the question that was pricking her insides, irritating and unpleasant, the way the bramble had been pricking her neck.

FOX'S BARGAIN

"WHERE IS EVERYONE ELSE?" BROOK ASKED. WHEN FOX DIDN'T answer right away, she said, "I mean—why are you all alone?"

Fox played with the fire. She got the idea he was looking for words.

"You could say I'm not a very friendly person, but that's not quite it." He frowned. "It's not that I don't like people. I do, I'm pretty social."

"Yeah, you are." And good thing, Brook thought. Otherwise I'd still be on the beach.

"I wish I could share the campsite with other kids," Fox said. "But being friendly gets you in trouble around here. I tried it for a while and it didn't go well. We ended up fighting so much that it got dangerous to stay together." He hesitated. "Did you ever read *Lord of the Flies*?"

She swallowed and shook her head no, wondering what he'd say.

"Well, it's a story about a bunch of kids on an island. The island isn't terrible. You get the idea they could've all worked together and had a pretty good time, but that's not what happens. By the time help gets there, they've split into tribes and started killing each other. It's a fight for survival. That's kind of what living here is like—except this island *is* terrible." Fox met her eyes. "It kind of changes your outlook on life," he said, being philosophical again.

Brook nodded. She knew he was telling the truth. She'd known as soon as she woke up on the cliffs, even though she hadn't wanted to believe it. The island *was* a terrible place. She also knew what kids could be like. The Children's Foundation was a different kind of island. Her life in Weed was an urban version of *Lord of the Flies*.

She'd known that for a while, ever since she'd found a tattered copy of the book dumped in a corner of Language Arts. She hadn't told Fox because she'd wanted to hear his version of the story. And now she knew: The island was bad, and the kids were bad—but why? Forget the details. Why any of it? Why would anyone, or anything, work so hard to bring a nobody like her to–

"What about you?" Fox pushed his hair back from his forehead.

Brook froze. "Me?"

"Tell me something about you. It doesn't have to be a big thing."

"Um, well, let's see." She ground a clump of moss to bits behind her back and tried to look thoughtful. No one ever asked Brook about herself. It made her head spin because what could she possibly say that wouldn't sound like a total sob story?

"Well, I'm an orphan, or I was." She gave a little laugh. "Nothing special, just another numbered file...in a building stuffed with numbered files. It was a fun, exciting life."

"Uh huh," Fox said. "What could possibly be more fun than being a number?"

She hoped it was a good performance, but she got the idea

he was wondering about her, which was the last thing she wanted—even though *she* was wondering about him too. Stuck in a bad story with someone she didn't understand.

Since he'd mentioned *The Lord of the Flies*, it made her curious who Fox thought he was. Did he see himself as the weak kid, Piggy, who got knocked off a cliff? Not likely. Maybe Rolf, Piggy's friend, who tried to help him and failed? She sure hoped not. Because who would that make her? But either of them would be better than the evil kid, Jack, who'd kill anyone who got in his way.

"You're cool, Brook," Fox said as if he could read her mind. "You're tough and smart, and I'm not flattering you, just calling it how it is. You seem like a what-you-see-is-what-you-get kind of girl. That's the only kind of friend worth having."

What you see is what you get? Brook thought. That's funny.

"Thanks," she said. "That's nice of you."

He spread his hands. "What I'm saying is, I—there's a word for it, but I forget—I—can *count on* you. Things are bad out there, and I'd like to have you on my team."

Brook pulled her knees to her chest. All at once she felt on edge, and it wasn't because of Fox's memory problems. "What does it mean to be on your team?" she said. You have the knife, she thought. You have the food and water and fire. What else will you want?

Fox nodded like he knew what she was thinking. "It means you have my back and I have yours. That's all. Two minds instead of one. We work together."

"Got it." Brook leaned back on her elbows, forcing herself to act casual. Stuck on an island, she thought, with a guy who probably thinks you're a weakling, and he wants you on his team. It's Rolf and Piggy all over again—except I'm not Piggy! The fire hissed and crackled at her feet. Fox was making sense, though. A team was a good idea.

Still, she might say no, because something about Fox said *caution*. But what kind of person would she want to team up with anyway? Someone who didn't make you nervous at all was probably a loser. Everyone worth knowing was a little dangerous. In a place like this, you *wanted* dangerous.

But that wasn't the real problem.

Brook saw the problem. Knew it inside and out.

She didn't want anyone.

Maybe she never had.

People weren't trustworthy. They said they loved you and wanted you until one day, without warning—they didn't. The love stopped. The care disappeared. Parents were blurry memories who didn't meet your eyes. It turned out you were just too much, way too much, and you found yourself stuck in the Children's Foundation, repeating the pattern over and over like a bad habit.

That's why it was better to be alone.

When she glanced across at Fox, he dropped his eyes like he saw the darkness in her thoughts. He wasn't pushing her, which was smart of him. The fire threw off sparks as he twisted the poker.

Maybe it's my fault, she thought, because I never wanted anyone in the first place. At least, not like I should. Not after that first time—maybe not even then. Maybe that's why they decided I wasn't good enough. The *caring* part of my heart is cracked, and caring is hard to fake, even when you try.

A team could maybe help with that.

Right then she decided she'd do it, she'd team up with Fox—but she wouldn't tell him for a while. She had to get her nerve up first.

What I really want, she thought, is what he has. A place where you can sit in a pool of sunlight and be quiet. Ideally there would be a door with a big lock. And you'd never have to leave until you wanted.

If she had a secret campsite all to herself, would she invite someone else to share it? She didn't think so. It would have to be a pretty special kid. Maybe that made Fox a better person, because he was willing to share this hidden place.

Sharing was better than nothing.

Probably.

Maybe.

"Why don't you sleep on it?" Fox said.

She forced a smile to her lips. "Good idea. It's been a long day. Gosh, what a stupid thing to say. I mean, it's been awhile since I've been dumped by a dragon. I'm out of practice."

Fox laughed. "Pleasure meeting you, Brook."

"Thanks," she said. "You too, Fox."

"See you in the morning. The moss behind you is pretty soft."

She brushed crumbled dirt off her fingers. Hopefully she'd be able to sleep. The idea of being on Fox's team was floating her insides up and down.

He gave her a little salute, got to his feet and moved into the shadows. She could barely see him as he curled up by the far rock wall. Sounds from the night moved closer: birdcalls, scurrying noises, the wind in the trees. The island pressed in, reminding her she had no clue what she was doing. How long should I sit here? she wondered. Should I pretend to be thinking things over? The idea made her a little panicky. *What if I come up with a reason to change my mind?*

Then she noticed something startling. The metal poker shone in the firelight, sharp and hooked. Fox had left it leaning in the flames. Not a big deal, she thought. He just forgot it. He's tired. But she knew that was ridiculous. Someone like Fox, who could barely stand to loan her a four inch knife, would never leave a deadly weapon glowing in the embers. She put an elbow on her knees and leaned her chin in one hand.

He is *trusting* you. That word, that idea he has such a hard time with—he's trying it.

You could grab that poker.

Nothing he could do.

Brook nodded to herself. The poker was the sign she'd been waiting for.

She'd be on his team. She wouldn't change her mind.

SCREAMS AND RUNNING

THE ANIMALS IN THE FOREST WERE CRAZY LOUD. IF BROOK HEARD this kind of noise in Weed, she'd think someone was dying. The screeches, hoots and shrieks sent her twisting to her knees in the night, digging at the moss for her shork until she remembered where she was. She could make out a few stars, pinpricking the sky in the patches that showed through branches. Once she heard a rumbling roar and something flew past, erasing stars as it went.

The dragon.

She crossed her arms over her chest and squeezed. No ceiling inches from your face, she told herself. No lumpy mattress, no unwashed bodies. No one creeping toward your bed. This is better, it's better.

But still bad.

When she finally slept, the screams of the forest followed her. She felt herself falling, hitting the floor. Felt herself lash out —felt herself run. She was always running in her dreams. Heart pounding, sneakers smacking, breath coming in ragged gulps. Brook was quick on her feet but it never mattered.

She'd start sprinting in an alley or a school parking lot. Even a playground. In the first burst of speed, her pursuers would vanish. But they always reappeared, moving closer without trying, like she was running in place while distance folded for them like a map so they could step across the city.

Her surroundings changed in a horrible, invisible way. She'd look over her shoulder or turn a corner and find herself in the one place she didn't want to be. Asphalt, linoleum, and grass melted to shadows, a room of locked closets, metal appliances and stained concrete. The chase always ended in the Children's Foundation basement.

The last place you'd ever want to be caught.

Brook came to, gasping. She pressed the back of her neck, smoothing away the tension, and huddled in the pitch darkness as something howled. Or maybe it was a wail. She didn't know her animal sounds. Maybe the dragon is circling, she thought. Who knows what sounds it makes? But he'll never find you here.

Over the dead fire, she couldn't make out Fox's shape in the dark. She put her cropped head back down on the moss and took slow, regular breaths. Pressing her shoulder into the ground, she tucked her knees and closed her eyes.

Remember where you are, she told herself.

Sharp golden sunlight hit her face. Her eyes snapped open on stone and moss and she sat up, blinking. Fox crouched by the fire, shoving charred wood to the center of the ring.

Giving her space.

Looking around in the light, she saw how hidden the camp was. If someone stood on the boulders overhead, he might still miss the sunken hollow. Leafy branches draped the tops of the rocks like a camouflage net. A couple of tree trunks stretched across like roof beams. Moss covered the ground like a thin green layer of memory foam, making things comfy. She didn't know if it was luck or hard work, but Fox's camp was perfectly tucked away.

She got to her feet feeling bruised and achy.

Fox gave her a nod. "Sleep ok? Sorry, bad question."

"Ha. You're right." She stepped to the spring-fed pool, knelt and cupped a drink, wishing she had her toothbrush. Her blurry outline in the water looked different, and she brushed her short hair with her fingertips. Her clothes were torn and dirty. Her shork was gone. So was her name.

Who are you? she thought.

It was like reaching for something, maybe a bird or butterfly, that always danced away. Effortless, not even trying, just out of reach. She knew her name was floating in her mind, but hidden so she'd never find it. She couldn't keep thinking about it, reaching for it. It would make her crazy.

She barely felt like herself at all.

"How hungry are you?" Maybe Fox sensed her mood because he didn't wait for an answer. "I've got more jerky, but today is a hunting day, so if you want to wait, we could cook something fresh. Or we could have a bite now and rabbit brunch."

Brook tried to pull her thoughts together. If she'd been alone, she would've pressed her back to the stone wall and slid down into the moss and held perfectly still until her mind and heart caught up. Instead, she took a breath through her nose and turned.

This was it.

"I'm in," she said. "About both things. What you said last night—let's be on a team. And also," she rushed on, "let's go hunting."

"Hey, excellent!" Fox grinned. "I'm happy you decided to stay. We'll make a good team—the best team, you'll see. And I love fresh rabbit."

A team! I'm on a team, she thought.

She smiled. Then she let herself laugh.

"Well of course you love fresh rabbits," she said, "I mean, haha, *every* fox would say that if foxes could talk."

Fox swept an arm out and dipped his head in a half bow. "I present to you the one and only talking fox."

Brook sighed. "Ah, laughing feels good."

"And it was just a little laugh," Fox pointed out.

That's as big as my laughs get, buddy, she could've said.

"I'll be ready in a minute." He shoved another chunk of smoking charcoal to the middle of the fire. The ash was deep and he was jabbing the poker around, searching for every last piece of glowing wood.

The poker.

Brook's eyes widened. What she'd mistaken for a poker in the night was really a long, serrated sword. The dark blade ended in a nasty hook. A loop of blackened twine was tied to the handle. It was hard to imagine a scarier-looking weapon. A kid could've ruled the Foundation with a thing like that.

Fox caught her staring. "Don't worry," he said. "It won't melt and I always clean it."

"Ah, that's a relief. It would be terrible if it got damaged." Brook looked away, then back at the sword. "Where did you get it? I mean—did the dragon give it to you or something?"

Fox hesitated.

Where are we? Brook thought. Did we travel back in time? If you put the clues together, would it be crazy to think we're stuck in the Dark Ages? Or back when pirates sailed the seas, burying treasure? She put a knuckle to her forehead.

Fox was watching her. "Actually," he said, "I found it."

She blinked. "You found it. Down a storm drain, buried in a dumpster, or what?"

He laughed and she felt relieved.

"I found it in the cliffs. Had to climb out on the rocks to get it."

Brook thought of the jagged, dirty rocks that ended in the belly of the sea. Kid-eating cliffs. Killer waves. She couldn't imagine someone climbing onto those rocks for anything.

Anything at all.

"I had to," Fox said. "Or someone else would have."

"That's impressive," she said after a minute.

You don't understand how bad this place is, she thought. Obviously you don't.

RABBIT HUNT

Brook paid close attention as they walked through a tangle of boulders and springy bushes that waited to slap her in the face. She didn't need more scrapes and bruises. There has to be a way to map the woods, she thought, memorize them like sidewalks and fire escapes.

Was the forest less scary in the morning? She wasn't sure. The trees didn't openly threaten her. But they weren't the bright, happy forests you saw on school posters with slogans that made you want to puke.

These woods were not playing around.

Trees fought over the ground in twisted clumps. Some of their fights must have been going on for decades, because trunks shoved each other back and forth, twisting their way into the sky. Selfish shrubs grabbed every spare inch of soil, disguising their thorns with pretty leaves. The morning light filtered through it all in a greenish haze. Each time Brook looked down, there were more burrs on her clothes and shoelaces. Cutting her hair off had been the right choice. Scratches were appearing on her bare legs. No wonder Fox wore pants.

All she had were jean shorts, and she felt jealous.

When they shoved their way out of the brush, it felt like escaping. Brook pinched dozens of burrs off her clothes before she remembered they'd be coming back the same way. The woods would get another chance at them—so she gave up and took in the scenery.

Fields of high grass rolled away toward the sand, tossing and swirling in the wind. The sun was a golden ball, hanging over the far-off dunes. She was glad they couldn't see the cliffs. Now she just needed to stop thinking about them. It was like letting the island win. She could imagine it gloating:

Can't get me out of your head, Brook, can you?

"Rabbits love these fields," Fox said, breaking the silence. "I've got a dozen snares. A bow and arrows would give them more of a fighting chance, but when you're hungry it's hard to care about sportsmanship."

"Poor bunnies," Brook said. "At least they have big families."

Fox shaded his eyes and scanned the open ground. Nothing moved that Brook could see. He led the way onto the plain, and she was happy to find that walking was easier in the high grass. She stretched out her arms and let the stalks and seedpods brush her fingertips. After the claustrophobic woods, the blue sky seemed huge. She decided that aside from their campsite, the fields were her favorite place on the island. They were open, honest. Even friendly.

So this place wasn't one hundred percent bad. *Take that, island.*

"Here's my first snare," Fox said. "I put them in the rabbit runs, where the little guys go back and forth. Ah, no luck."

Brook leaned close. In an area of flattened turf, a loop of twine hung from a frame made of sticks. The lasso was empty.

"Do these actually work?" she asked.

"Of course they do," Fox said.

She realized she'd offended him. "How cool," she said. "Super resourceful."

Fox stared down at the trap. "Rabbits jump through the slip-knot in the dark and...ahhk." He put a hand to his neck.

Brook thought about bunnies nibbling clover and felt a little guilty. But she also felt hungry. Getting hungrier.

"Have I mentioned this is genius?" she said.

Fox scoffed. Then he gave up and smiled.

But the next snare was empty too. And the third one.

"It's a numbers game," Fox said.

The fourth and fifth and sixth were empty. He muttered under his breath.

"It's ok," Brook said. "No rush."

Luckily, the seventh held a dead rabbit. A nice big one, Brook thought. And good thing. Fox's jaw had been getting harder, his eyes darker. She didn't want to see him lose his cool.

"About time," he said. "I usually do better than this." He rubbed his chin. "Makes you wonder if the rabbits are catching on."

The slipknot on the eighth trap had been jerked to one side, like something had struggled and pulled free. The ninth was empty again.

"It's just bad luck," Brook said.

Fox kicked at grass stems as he walked, making twice as much noise as usual. Brook hoped he wasn't mad about feeding her, because what was she supposed to do, volunteer to leave? Good thing we're officially on a team, she was thinking—when they rounded a bend in the faint path and Fox stopped short.

The jerky energy left his body. He got very still.

"What is it?" Brook whispered. "Did you catch another?"

She leaned around him to see. The rabbit run entered a patch of high red grass. Some kind of special edition grass like you'd see in a rich person's yard. Then she saw the broken snare —cracked sticks and snapped twine. The snare was red, and so was the dirt and everything, even the gravel. Brook realized she was looking at blood. It must've sprayed out from the trap or been wildly smeared around. For a second, she saw blood drip-drip-dripping onto a dirty concrete floor.

She shuddered and looked down, focusing on the trampled soil and bent grass.

Then she stepped away from the blood—and away from Fox.

Brook knew the signs. Anger can build and build inside you until even when you try to hold it in, you've hardly got a chance. When you see that coming in another person, you get out of the way if you have any brains at all. But Fox surprised her.

He didn't cuss or stomp on the broken trap or turn to yell at her. Instead, his hand dropped to his knife and he turned in a slow circle, searching the plain. It made the center of her stomach go very still. Fox glanced back the way they'd come. His eyes got narrow.

"We'd better get to the trees," he said.

Cold wind traced Brook's spine. "Ok," she said, and waited for him to move. She wasn't going to be left behind. Fox glided away from the bloody circle, and Brook lengthened her strides to keep up.

"What did that?" she asked, not caring if Fox was on edge. She felt exposed. Tricked. She'd thought the fields were pretty and bright, but now they felt deadly, a place you crossed as quickly as you could. Fox hadn't offered her a weapon. He had the sword *and* the knife. Maybe he'd thought they wouldn't need them, but now she felt almost naked, like she'd been dropped in a low-light parking garage without even a shiv or a winter coat.

"What did that?" she said again, drawing even with Fox.

"I'll tell you," he said, "when we reach the trees. Let's keep our voices down."

She didn't care for that answer, but she balled up her fists and kept pace, arranging her thoughts as they hurried through whispery, wind-tossed grass that was tall enough to hide an awful lot. Her left hip ached. Dry seedpods rattled like tiny, hollow drums.

Blood all over the place, she thought. Something shredded that rabbit like nothing. You're holding back things I should know and we're supposed to be on a team. You can't treat me that way, pal. No way. I'm not your little sidekick. You're angry, huh? Well, so am I.

I wish I had my shork.

SPILLING GUTS

BY THE TIME THEY REACHED THE EDGE OF THE FOREST, BROOK'S fingers had bit into her palms, leaving white half-circles. She couldn't afford to go crazy on Fox, but that didn't mean she'd let this slide. Not a chance. In the shadow of the trees, she slid her hands to her hips.

Fox looked back over the fields. A few clouds moved in the blue sky, but otherwise nothing had changed. When the boy turned to face her, she began counting down from ten. She'd give him a chance to tell her what was going on. Ten, nine, eight, seven, six, five, four…

"Death Dogs," Fox said.

She forgot her number.

"I don't think they're a normal species," he said. "Maybe you'd call them monsters. They're like wolves, with teeth and fur and they hunt in packs, but they also have stingers."

"How—do you know?" Brook said.

Fox turned and looked hard in her eyes. "Because I've seen them." He hesitated. "I've seen them kill. It's awful. They hunt at night, usually, but you can't be too careful. If they catch you in open country, it's over."

"So—we're safe now?" Brook said.

Fox gestured at the trees. "Yeah. Anyway, if they'd picked up our scent, they'd already be here."

Brook started another countdown, slower this time. She needed it for herself. Ten...nine...eight...seven...six...five...four...three...two...one.

Fox was staring across the fields like the conversation was over.

"Who do you think you are?" she said. "You acted like we were taking a walk in the park. That was a joke, a dirty joke. I could've been ripped apart by dogs and you didn't even warn me." *Or give me a knife.*

She put her hands behind her back. They were shaking—not with fear but with anger. If she wasn't careful, she'd say or do something she'd regret.

Fox crossed his arms and studied a patch of shadow.

"Ok," he said. "You've got a point, but here's the thing. I didn't expect Death Dogs this far inland. I haven't seen any signs and I didn't think I was putting you in danger, no more than waking up on this"—he scowled—"this hunk of rock. I thought the rabbits would be easy, and I didn't want to dump everything on you at once. It's a lot to handle, so believe it or not, I was trying to help."

She felt frustrated when she couldn't find any holes in his answer, but at the same time, she was pretty sure that when you were on a team, you didn't hold all kinds of secrets back.

"Maybe you shouldn't try so hard," she said. "Maybe I can handle more than you think. Anything else you were waiting to tell me?"

Fox's eyes burned into hers. He blinked. Then he sighed. "You know about the dragon," he said. "I mentioned the castle and the blue-faces. They're vicious but they keep to themselves. Why wouldn't they, when they have everything they need? There are probably other nasty creatures on the island, but the Death Dogs are the ones I know about. Other than that..." He shrugged, but Brook knew the look too well to be fooled.

"What else?"

"Just—other kids," Fox said. "Feral, I guess you could call them. Some of them are really dangerous. Luckily there are two of us now, but we'll keep an eye out."

"Oh," she said. "Fantastic."

No one ever spilled all their guts. There was always something left, and it was usually slimy. She looked at him, then away. Her stomach felt flat and achy.

"I'm sorry, Brook," Fox said. "I let you down. I should've known better because you're sharp, which is one reason I liked you in the first place. I shouldn't have treated you like a kid. Give me another chance, ok?"

When she looked up, his face had softened. She was almost surprised to hear herself say:

"Well, ok, I guess."

She couldn't help it. Apologies were rarer than birthday cards at the Foundation.

"Great." Fox let out a breath, rubbing his hands together. He pushed his hair off his forehead and turned in a half-circle. "Cool."

He may be a jerk but he's glad you're here, Brook thought, and had to keep herself from smiling.

"How about lunch, or brunch, whatever this is?" Fox said. "We could do something I hardly ever do, make a fire in the woods—a very small one, with hardly any smoke, you know? And cook this rabbit. Then I could make it up to you by showing you something cool, like one of the beaches—or even the castle."

His eyes always got a little bigger when he mentioned the castle.

"Yes, please," she said, putting some bounce in her voice.

"That sounds amazing." She needed to get back on Fox's good side.

She watched him slice open the rabbit. It was gross but she'd seen worse things, and anyway, it was edible. She'd cut up raw chicken on kitchen duty in the Foundation, always closely supervised, since God forbid that anyone steal a kitchen knife or mess up dinner, no matter what happened after curfew. The rabbit was cuter than a chicken, and it had more blood, but she was so hungry she didn't care.

She only looked away once, when Fox cut off its head.

"Nice and fresh," he said, stripping away the fur. "We'll roast it."

Fox handed her the knife like a peace offering, and she cut some thin branches off a tree and sharpened the ends to points. They slid chunks of raw rabbit onto the skewers and turned them over the small blaze Fox built. The meat took longer to cook than Brook would've liked.

"Can we eat it medium-rare?" she asked.

Fox laughed. "It's the best you can hope for, unless you like it black."

He showed her how to turn the meat slowly over the fire to keep it from going up in flames. As soon as the fire gave them embers, they used those.

"Steadier heat," Fox said. "Less likely to burn."

By the time the first pieces had cooled enough to eat, Brook's mouth was watering. The sizzling rabbit smelled wonderful. She and Fox tore off bites with their teeth. The meat was a little tough—"from running for its life," Fox said—but delicious. In fact, Brook felt like she'd eaten it before, many times. Usually baked, sometimes in soup with noodles, and once or twice fried with bread crumbs.

"I can't believe it tastes like chicken," she said. "But more earthy."

Fox nodded. "Kind of crazy, right?—certain things you can't escape from."

"Ha!" she said, because *escaping from chicken*. But he was right, certain things followed you wherever you went, and most of them were a lot worse than chicken. After they ate, Brook did her best to wipe the grease off her hands, but it was a losing battle. She hated feeling dirty, and it probably wasn't going to get better. At least her stomach was full. For now, anyway. They'd eaten the entire rabbit.

"What will it be?" Fox leaned against a tree trunk and picked his teeth with a little bone, somehow making it seem not-creepy. "The beach? A forest overlook? The castle?"

It was so obvious what he wanted that Brook smiled.

"Hmm, let's see. I was thinking it would be great to have a look at..." She studied the branches overhead, faking thoughtfulness. "How about the beeea—actually, no."

Fox looked relieved.

"I'd enjoy a nice overlook."

"Ok." He nodded sadly.

"Just kidding. Show me the castle."

His eyebrows shot up. "Really? Cool. Wait, am I that obvious?"

"Like an open book," Brook said, wishing it was true.

THE CASTLE

They wove along the edges of the woods, dodging green plants that looked all innocent but were packing stingers. Brook had the Death Dogs in the back of her mind, and she was sure Fox did too. Otherwise, they would've just walked across the fields. Instead, they hugged the tree line for cover as they hiked, dodging the branches trying to claw them. Sunlight through the leaves left blotches on her skin like gray-green camo.

"This is like walking an invisible balance beam," Brook said.

It took Fox a second to get it, then he smiled. "This balance beam is heading north, in case you're wondering," he said. "Toward the center of the island."

"The heart of the mystery," Brook said.

Fox tapped his forehead as he dodged a thorn bush. "You've got a philosophical streak too."

"You're not wrong," Brook said. "I wonder about things, but it hasn't done me a whole lot of good."

"Tell me about it," Fox said.

They shared a smile—maybe even a smirk.

This guy's ok, Brook thought.

Balancing on the edges of the forest, they snuck along for a while.

A dozen football fields. Maybe a mile. Or even two.

Brook wasn't great at gauging distances. She wished she wasn't such a city girl. From the Children's Foundation to Weed Middle School was as good as her distance measurements got, and all she knew was how long it took her to make the trip. Eight minutes—five minutes if she fast-walked—always alone, with an eye out for trouble. She and Fox had been hiking for about fifteen minutes, mostly in silence, except for "watch that branch," and "look out, thorny thing," when Fox turned left, into the woods.

"The castle is in the woods?" Brook said.

"You'll see."

"Please don't tell me it's made of trees."

Back in the deeper shadow, the forest sloped up. The ground got rocky and after a few minutes their feet hit solid stone. Edging along boulders, watching her shins, Brook thought about how useless her thin sneakers were. Filthy, wet, falling apart. No protection, and they made her do everything in slow motion. Oh well. Going slow was better anyway.

There were kids who strutted around trying to prove themselves. *Hey, check me out.* Working hard to show they were just as dangerous as anyone else. And unless they had a gang behind them, those kids ended up with casts and stitches. No thanks. Calm, cool and in control was better—always.

Even so, she stole a glance at Fox's kicks as she skidded around. Tough-looking, with grippy treads for hiking. Even kind of stylish. Who was this guy, that he got such good stuff? She grabbed a boulder as her feet started to slide out from under her like they were covered in butter. Darn it, now she felt jealous. Some kids would kill for Fox's shoes, and if this went on much longer, she'd be one of them.

"Hey Fox, nice kicks," she said.

"Thanks, Brook. Hey, don't fall off the side, ok?"

"Ooo, great tip." *But I'm having so much fun on my roller skates.* She wondered how he'd lucked out with his shoes, and more important, what would happen to her when the rest of her clothes started falling apart like her flimsy canvas knockoffs. Maybe she should start saving rabbit skins.

Then she had to pay attention to the climb, searching for finger holds to keep herself from skidding down the giant slabs. Fox stayed within an arm's reach, keeping an eye on her. When she caught him hovering, he shrugged and raised his eyebrows.

"I'd hate to lose you on your first day."

"I'm *fine*." Brook frowned at him, then toppled forward and grabbed a rock ledge as her feet shot out from under her with a squelching sound.

"Ok, you're fine." Fox held up his hands.

Brook pulled herself upright. "It's no different than gym class—or climbing a fire escape," she said through gritted teeth.

"Wow," Fox said. "Your gym classes must be wild. And your fire escapes must be covered in banana peels."

"Curse you," Brook said.

He really thinks I'm a klutz, she thought. Great. These trash shoes, though!

When she jumped off the last boulder and onto solid ground, she shoved her cropped hair out of her face, arched her arms in a stretch, and wriggled her battered fingers.

"Phew, glad that's over."

Fox's smile looked smug.

Let him think what he wants. Scuffing her feet over pine needles, she followed him through scratchy evergreens—and froze. They stood on the edge of a cliff. Sun-baked rock dove forty or fifty feet to the open plain below, where chunks of rock littered the ground. It would be a fatal fall—but at least this cliff didn't try to ambush you. Not like the coast with its slick and hungry teeth.

Looking down at the high brown grass, flattened here and there by rock, she realized that's where they'd be if they'd stuck to the open ground. Blocked from the woods by flat, unclimbable stone. It would've been like standing in a trashy courtyard with a project building at your back. Nowhere to run. Nowhere to hide.

Then she looked further out and saw the castle.

"Oh my—whoa."

Fox nodded. "Right?"

She shaded her eyes against the midday glare.

The castle sprawled huge and strong and dark against the plains, giving off a wealthy vibe, the kind of place that could never be built again because big blocks of stone were so expensive. It made her feel tiny, even standing miles away. She could make out arched windows that probably opened on pent houses or executive suites. The thick, regular notches at the tops of the walls had all kinds of swagger.

And the towers!—Brook let out a long, low breath. Five of them rose high and graceful into the blue sky, one on each corner and the fifth one in the middle. If you lived in one of *those*, you'd feel like you were someone.

She found herself staring with a hand over her mouth.

Yeah, I'm the biggest thing on this island, the castle seemed to say. I'm in charge and I'm not apologizing, so don't tick me off.

Brook loved it instantly. Maybe the killer cliffs and hungry ocean and the dragon didn't get the last laugh with everyone after all.

These walls are made to keep danger out, she thought. Not like the Children's Foundation, made to seal nastiness in. She'd assumed the castle would be a pile of stones, some kind of glorified hide-out.

Now she pictured herself throwing a—what did you call those clawed hooks?—one of those over a wall, and pulling herself up a rope in the moonlight. Then tiptoeing up tower stairs, winding higher and higher into the stars. She'd walk down a stone hall, turn into an open doorway, and there it would be.

A clean, quiet room with a view. She'd lock the door behind her and lower herself into a pool of moonlight, soft and silver. She'd rest. She'd think. She'd dream. All by herself, for as long as she wanted. After a while the sun would rise and the pool of moon would turn to warm, liquid gold and she'd–

"Amazing, isn't it," Fox said.

She gave a little twitch.

"Has to be at least two acres inside," he said. "Everything they need in there, a water source, gardens, shelter, even chickens. It's the perfect set-up."

Brook shook her head. "How do you know?"

"Those are the rumors," Fox said. "And look at the place. Can you imagine anything less? Besides, the blue-face kids never leave. The time I knocked on the door, they didn't even come out to fight. Just threw rocks down at me and laughed. They're self-sufficient."

They stared across the plain.

"How can we get in?" Brook said.

Fox had been tapping his knife on a stone. He turned to look at her.

"Wow, Brook. You don't mess around."

No joke, she thought. Look at us, we're on Death Island.

"But you're thinking the same thing, right?" she said.

Getting inside the castle was her one big goal. It had happened in a couple seconds, which made it a rushed decision, but she couldn't help it. The castle was the place for her—it was obvious, like a light clicking on in a dark room. She needed to get there. Whoever had put her on the island should never have let her see the castle, never even let the *idea* of the castle cross her mind, because now she'd do whatever she had to. She couldn't push Fox, though. She had to coax him along and help him see it her way.

"I don't know." Fox was staring out over the fields. "If we really want to try and get in, we'll have to do some serious thinking. Some serious planning. It would be like one of those heist movies where there's a billion dollars or some priceless blueprint in a safe, but if one little thing goes wrong, everyone dies. And in a movie, everyone's ok with that, but in real life–"

"I get it," Brook said. "But you don't think I'm crazy. Admit it, you want to get in there too, at least a little bit."

Fox licked his lips and turned to look her. "Well, sure I do. I mean, if you're stuck out here, how couldn't you? Once you got inside, you wouldn't have to worry about the dragon or the Death Dogs, or hunting—nothing. You do a few chores to keep things running, then you sit back and take it easy. But Brook— don't set your heart on it, ok?"

Brook smiled. She had a hard time seeing Fox taking it easy. She could definitely see him patrolling the walls or keeping an eye on the island from the top of a tower, though.

"Set my heart on it?" She laughed. "C'mon, Fox, I'm not a kindergartner asking for a lollipop."

"Good point. I guess you're not covered in sparkles."

"Nope," Brook said. "Not me." Although she wouldn't have minded a *few* sparkles. At the Foundation, wearing anything bright or glittery was asking to get slapped.

"Well, happy you like the castle," Fox said. "Alone, I never had a chance to get inside, but together—who knows, Brook, who knows? Maybe we'll figure something out. Those blue-faces have had everything their way for so long, they'll never see it coming. Maybe our luck is about to change."

"Lightning from a clear sky," Brook said. "That's us."

"Nice," Fox said. "Or like bats out of hell."

She sniffed and decided to lay it on thick. "Fox, has it ever occurred to you that hell is red, not black? Because—all that fire. Bats flying out of hell would be pretty easy to see. Maybe go with 'bats out of the dark' next time. Or 'bats out of the night.' Either one would be better."

"What the heck, Brook." Fox laughed. "You're over the top."

"Bats out of hell, seriously?"

They were both in a good mood, which was what she needed. For this to work, Fox had to like her and take her seriously. She was glad he was coming around.

Because aside from being dropped into the castle out of a jet or using—what were they called, grapples? No, grappling hooks, crazy stuff that only worked in heist movies—she didn't see a single way to get inside.

STRANGER ON THE PLAIN

"Sooo, have you seen any adults around?" Brook asked.

They crunched quietly along the edges of the woods, feeling pretty good after their chat about the castle. Brook was doing her best to keep feeling that way.

"Not a single one," Fox said. "If there were grown-ups, there'd be rules and some kind of escape plan. Huge bonfires, people building rafts. Believe me, there's none of that, makes it too easy to get picked off. No adults, no rules, no big plans. None."

Brook was relieved there were no grown-ups because if there were, they'd be creating schedules, putting kids on work teams, all that fake-important stuff. And it would be the Foundation all over again. The mean kids would kiss up and keep doing whatever they wanted. Meanwhile, the adults would kick back in the castle, gossiping and watching their soap operas while all hell broke loose. It was way better to have everything out in the open.

It meant Team Brook-Fox had a shot at the castle.

Brook was having a hard time getting the castle out of her

head. She knew there was no point in imagining what the rooms would look like, or wondering how it would be to have a garden that didn't wilt and die in the city heat. But she couldn't seem to help herself. She swatted a low-hanging branch aside.

"Did you ever go swimming, Fox? You know, in a pool?"

"Don't think so. As far as I remember."

"Me either, pretty sure. Maybe the castle has one."

"Heck yeah, it's big enough."

She pictured a freshwater spring bubbling into an enclosure as big as an aquatic center—with a garden crowding the edges. Everyone knew vegetables were good for you. Maybe she'd like them if she got the chance. The only ones she'd tried were carrot sticks with ranch, slimy green beans and watery, tasteless lettuce.

"Hey Foxy, think there's a garden in there?"

"Gotta be with all that space...*Brooklyn.*"

"Brooklyn? Very funny, but let's stick with Brook."

Brooklyn sounded like a girl who had a college fund and earrings by the time she could walk. Anyone named Brooklyn would get pulverized in Weed. And Brooklyn would definitely not get her hands and knees dirty, working in a castle garden. Brooklyn would not deserve this castle the way Brook did.

"So, do Foxes eat vegetables?"

"Is that a serious question?"

"Haha."

At the Foundation and Weed Middle School, there'd been plenty of junk to eat. A steady diet of rolled-up pizza and chocolate milk wasn't good for you, but it kept you going. Out here, the stakes were higher. Brook thought unlimited veggies and chicken—Fox said there were chickens—would be a huge advantage. She was ready to change her diet and never look back. Shoot, she was ready to change her life. All she needed was the castle to give her a fighting chance.

"Hey Fox, ever been inside a henhouse?"

"Nope, don't think I—oh my gosh, Brook, you've gotta stop." He chuckled.

She took a moment to enjoy her funniness as they circled a patch of thorns. The sun was over the forest now, casting spiky shadows on their skins.

Now let's see. The castle was more than just amenities. It would give them shelter when it stormed, like her first night on the cliffs. It would give them a bunker when the dragon came inland—no need to worry about a dragon when you've got a castle. No need to watch your back at all, except from about a mile in the air. Free time to relax in the pool or in a quiet corner.

But best of all...

She kept returning to the safe, bright room at the top of a tower. It seemed too good to be true. So much so that she couldn't even joke with Fox about it.

You're being dumb, she told herself. You don't even know that room exists.

But with Fox backing her up, maybe Team B-F could get inside. And maybe, just maybe, when she climbed the stairs, the room would be there, waiting.

You've never had a dangerous friend, she thought. Never had a friend other people would listen to. Wow, that would've changed things. Not that you and Fox are friends—at least not yet—but you're a team. People can't walk all over you now. They have to take you seriously, not talk down to you, not force you into situations.

All this time, they'd been weaving along the balance beam at the edge of the woods, walking a line between the salty, windswept grass and the greenish shade of the trees. Free to move but not too obvious. Hidden, but not attacked by leaves and twigs.

Brook tried to think of another Fox joke.

Whoa, slow down, she told herself. You had one good lunch and you saw a castle and just like that, you think the whole world is gonna change. Get a grip. But she couldn't help it if she felt good.

Then Fox stopped so suddenly she bumped into him. "Oof." She caught herself and slid away in case he took a swing. But he didn't even notice.

"Out there," he said, pointing toward the plain. "Look."

He crouched in the scrub and Brook got down beside him.

Sure enough, out in the sunlight and waving grass, she caught movement. Wind tossed her chopped hair against her chin as she shaded her eyes. Far out in the flatlands, light gleamed on a small upright figure. His legs, hidden by the grass, had to be moving fast.

"It's another kid," Brook said.

Fox nodded but didn't speak.

"Should we go out there and talk?" she said.

Fox shook his head no. "With any luck, he hasn't noticed us."

"If he has, so what?"

All the fun drained out of their conversation.

"I'm not sure you've been paying attention." Fox crossed his arms. "Just about anything you meet on this island will kill you, and that includes other kids."

"But—but we're together."

He didn't smile. "I took a calculated risk with you, Brook. It paid off, but I had the edge. I saw you before you saw me and I took a good long look to make sure you weren't a threat. Even after you woke up and we talked, it still took me a while to decide you were ok. You can't just walk up to people here."

She nodded, feeling offended but knowing it was true. She didn't like the idea of Fox spying on her while she slept. But she would've done the same, she guessed, if she'd come across his battered body. She might have even frisked him to see if he was carrying a weapon. Would that have made her a jerk?

"So we just let him wander around out there?" she said.

"Here's the thing," Fox said. "We don't know he's wandering. We don't know how long he's been on the island or whether he's working alone." He hadn't taken his eyes off the distant figure, steadily moving closer. "Let's get out of sight."

"And watch from the trees?" Brook said.

Fox was already sliding into the forest on his hands and knees. She blew hair out of her face and followed, trying to make sense of it. If anything, the solitary kid in the tall grass had spooked Fox more than the Death Dogs. It didn't add up.

In the shadow of the forest, Fox stood behind a tree trunk, looking back.

"Heading right this way," he muttered. "Like he knows we're here."

"Would it hurt to yell? You know, from a distance?" Brook honestly wasn't sure. Fox was nervous and that made her nervous. Some kids were pure poison, it was true. You didn't want to mess with them, nod at them, get their attention in any way. Monique at the Foundation had been like that, with a posse waiting to follow her lead. Whoa, Monique—she'd remembered a name.

"Maybe we should leave," Brook said.

"Still coming our way," Fox said. "Let's lose him before he gets any closer, huh?"

"Yeah, let's."

When Fox trotted away, dodging trees and ducking under vines, she stayed right on his heels, even though her hip flared up and her shoes kept slipping. For another minute, if she looked over her shoulder, she could see flashes of the stranger getting closer to the edge of the sunny field. He didn't slow down at all, just kept coming like he'd been shot out of a gun.

It was creepy.

Then the leafy green maze of the forest took them out of sight. If the kid was trying to intersect them, they'd be long gone by the time he was in the woods.

Well, maybe not long gone.

But safely gone.

Gone enough.

She hoped.

BROOK VERSUS WOODS

AS THEY BURROWED INTO THE TREES, THE COLORS CHANGED. Fresh greens faded to fatigue and olive. Shadows thickened from charcoal sketches to pools of oil. The forest got deep and dark faster than Brook would've liked.

As she plunged after Fox, she thought, *How many kids are on Death Island? And how many are bad and how can you know who is who?* Maybe the boy behind them was a survivor like her, and he needed help. Then a spider with mile-long legs swung past her face, and she told herself to snap out of it. She focused on the thorns and thickets, the filtered greenish light, and Fox's retreating back. He barely ever slowed, shoulders upright, legs pumping, light on his feet.

Well, he is called Fox, she thought. What did you expect? Then she thought, You need to get a handle on the forest too. Don't let it boss you. Right now, your only chance if you lost Fox would be to climb a tree and hug a branch all night. Is that what you want?

So she started to push herself in small ways. Keeping her pace the same as his, she veered a little to the right, a little to the left, and back—like he was an arrow, flying straight ahead, and she was a—well, something just as fast but with more freedom. Something learning the forest, something not afraid. Her path fluttered back and forth behind Fox. *Maybe a high-speed butterfly.* She swerved around bogs, jumped over knobby roots, side-stepped vines like they were partners in a dance. She did it quietly, and Fox didn't look back.

These woods, she decided, are the nasty kind, but I'm getting their number. All I need is a little more time. Fox is right, bad things happen in the open. Death Dogs, dangerous kids patrolling in fast straight lines. If you go out there, anyone can see you, and then there's the wind, whipping your smell around—yeah, I definitely smell now—and the Death Dogs can sniff you out. She did her best to *not* think about the dragon.

Then she realized she was tired of running. Her hip ached, her lungs burned—she had to stop fluttering around. As she struggled to keep Fox in sight, she imagined the island laughing at her, a hateful laugh that rumbled down the coast like crashing waves, echoing in hidden caves beneath her feet. Jagged slivers of light through the trees made her think the island was smiling.

Brook wiped her forehead with a dirty hand. "I'm fine," she whispered. A hollow knocking rang through the woods and she cocked her head, trying to locate the sound. *Hmm.* It sounded like the water pipes in the Foundation's walls. But there wasn't any plumbing in the–

"Eee-eee!" A red-headed bird swooped at her with an eerie cry.

Brook gasped and ducked, shielding her face as the bird shot past. She caught a glimpse of an open beak, serrated like a steak knife. Five heartbeats later, she was still hunched over, one hand hovering by her eyes.

Bloodthirsty birds, she thought. Are you kidding me? This place wants to get the jump on you. It's waiting for an opening. So stay awake, like you're on the streets in Weed. After a while your street smarts will turn into woods smarts, but it will take some work.

And she knew she wasn't ready for this yet. Without Fox she'd be totally clueless. *If I lose track of this guy, or if he gets tired of me, I'm as good as dead.*

I've gotta keep him close.

I have to. At least for now.

She didn't like the thought one bit. It made her frown as she scuffed through dead leaves, trying to catch her breath. And it made her wonder why he'd chosen her for his team. What if he wasn't as tough as she thought? *Because let's be real, him running from that boy in the field was weird.*

She hadn't expected that, not at all. Fox didn't seem like the retreating kind. Maybe she'd been wrong about him, maybe he wasn't so dangerous—even though he had a sharp knife and a scary sword, and seemed comfortable with both.

Ahead of her, Fox swerved right to avoid a thicket. She went left, showing the forest she wasn't scared, even though she was losing speed. When she reached an open patch of woods on the far side, Fox had ghosted ahead. *Does he ever slow down?*

Then she thought, He's dangerous all right, even if you haven't seen him do anything. When your hair was in the thorns and he held up the knife—you thought he might cut your throat. That's not how you feel about a nice, safe person.

She shoved another whip-thin branch away from her eyes and plunged through *another* patch of clingy plants. Her feet felt packed in dirt.

Nice and safe he is not, she thought. Dangerous and sort of honest, yes. So give it a rest. He knows all kinds of things you don't know yet, so if he wants to run into the woods, you run into the woods. You've only been here a day. And hey, it's always smart to avoid a fight if you can. She winced and forced herself into a jog. All of a sudden, her knees felt rusty.

Gritting her teeth, she sped up to close the distance between them. She jumped over a patch of marshy ground, but she came down in a sloppy skid, arms flailing. One of her feet glopped into wet mud, and when she pulled free, her shoe and half her shin were slimy black.

"Blech."

A second later, both her feet shot out from under her. "Aah!" She caught herself with her hands, her face inches from the dirt. Centipedes writhed from under her fingers like tiny monsters. *Yikes yikes yikes!*

Fox stepped from behind a tree as she thrashed around. He jogged back to her. "Hey, Brook." Very casual, like he wasn't watching her self destruct.

She struggled to her feet, flicking her fingers like a crazy person.

"You ok?" he asked.

Oh yeah, wrestling bugs in the mud is amazing, she wanted to say.

Instead she gulped a breath and gave him a thumbs-up. *Don't mind me. Doing great.*

He took a long look at her.

Slimy legs, dirty face, sorta-hyperventilating.

Perfect.

"Need to take a breather, Brook?"

She swallowed. "Nope, good to go."

"Ok." He moved forward at a walk.

She wondered if he was rolling his eyes.

A few minutes ago, she'd been cracking Fox jokes. Then the island had come after her, and the red-headed bird may as well have started pecking on her chest: Knock, knock, knock. Fox, fox, fox. Team Brook-Fox was really Team Fox-Brook.

Or maybe just Team Fox.

It was a good thing he'd decided to like her.

And maybe a little strange.

UNWANTED

"Penny for your thoughts, Brook." Fox looked back. "I think it's safe to talk now."

Oh great. And at the same time, what a relief.

She shoved her hands in her shallow pockets and tried to pull herself together. "Cool," she said. "Umm." What could she say? *Well, Fox, since you asked, I've been thinking about* you. She reached for a joke, but she couldn't find one so instead she blurted out, "What do you think this place is?"

A big question. A dumb question. A philosophical, black hole of a question.

Fox gave a low whistle. "I wish I knew, Brook. I wish I knew."

She snapped off a fern leaf and fanned her burning face. It probably made her look stupid but she didn't care.

"I'm not sure where I'm from." Fox started hiking, politely acting like he hadn't noticed her little breakdown. "Don't have a lot of memories," he said, "so I don't have much to work with. For example, I'm not sure if the weather here is weird."

Brook fell into step behind him, willing her pulse back to

normal. "I don't think the weather is weird." She was happy he'd picked an easy topic. "It feels like California."

"So we could be in America."

"We could be. Except."

"Except the dragon."

"Right." She brushed back her hair and instantly regretted it because her hands were so dirty. "And the castle." She dodged a black beetle as big as her fist, clicking its jaws and wobbling toward her ankles. Apparently the whole forest was coming after her now. But at least they'd stopped running. At least now they could talk, and she didn't have to be stuck in her head. She stepped up onto a dry log and walked on top, safe from creepy crawlies.

"My theory," she said, "since I know you'd love to hear it, is that we're a few hundred years in the past—the Dark Ages, when monsters roamed the earth."

"Nice," Fox said. "I like that theory. It explains the dragon." He stopped abruptly, like something inside him had twisted and turned into a hook. "Someone would still have to shove us in a time machine though," he said, "*after* they erased our memories —so it's still horrible on purpose. Nothing changes that."

"Horrible on purpose. Yeah." Brook took a few more steps, keeping her balance and thinking, *Well, of course it's on purpose.*

Fox laughed, but the laugh didn't sound quite right.

"What's wrong?" Brook finally said. If she pretended not to notice the awkward laugh, well, Fox *would* notice and store it away for the day when he took a close look at her and decided whether to keep her around.

"My old life," Fox said.

She waited.

"You don't remember your name," he said.

She shook her head.

"Neither do I. But in my case, I never had a name. No one

gave me one. I was never wanted. Never wanted, ever. That's all I know about who I was. It hangs around in your bones."

Brook felt like all the air had been sucked out of the forest. Her feet felt heavy. She didn't ask how Fox knew he was never wanted. That didn't matter. Instead she licked her dry lips and said, "I'm sorry." And she was. She knew what it felt like to be unwanted, except in her case, she'd been wanted once and then never again.

She wasn't sure which would be worse.

She jumped off her log to walk beside Fox. He didn't seem to mind.

Then her stomach jolted. *WAIT*. She forced herself to keep moving as her whole body tightened. *What if...what if that's who gets sent here? Rejects no one wants. What if the island is a place for kids like us? And the blue-faces in their castle, they're the only ones who belong. The island is theirs, but instead of helping people like me and Fox, they fight to stay in charge, to keep us out, to keep us...unwanted.*

The idea took her breath away. And it made her feel silly, because the truth was so obvious. She squeezed her fingers, making and unmaking fists.

Death Island is Reject Island.

As a rule, Brook tried not to feel sorry for herself, not if she could help it. But all of a sudden she felt sorry for Fox, and she had a sneaky feeling she was feeling sorry for herself at the same time.

I feel sorry for him. I feel sorry for us.

Being unwanted made you feel far away and too close at the same time. It made you numb and crazy and twisted up inside.

It was the worst feeling in the world.

THERE'S NO NORMAL

By the time they made it back to the campsite, Brook's shoes were full of slime and leaf mold. In Weed, the cheap sneaks might have lasted months. Here they were used up in a few hours. She sat down in a bed of moss, leaned against the rock wall and yanked them off. Her socks were muddy brown. She pulled them off, holding her breath, and groaned.

Who knows how long I've had these on, she thought. Days for sure. Sorry, feet.

She wriggled her wrinkled toes in the gray-gold light, surprised how good it felt—and how tired she was. The sun still hovered over the trees, but she was ready to curl up. She wished she had a blanket, and that made her picture the castle again. The kids in there had blankets, blankets they didn't even need. The kids in there had everything, and they did their best to never share.

"Hungry?" Fox was digging at the cold fire, shoving coals around. He had a knack for finding embers in the ash. Brook had never kindled a fire in her life, and it was fascinating to watch him.

"Just a little hungry," Brook said. "No hurry." She wouldn't mind a piece of rabbit jerky, but she didn't want Fox to stop messing with the fire. The air was starting to get cold, and she felt the chill between her shoulder blades. The island was shutting down for the night, getting ready to wrap itself in dark and monsters. She scooted closer to the fire as wisps of smoke began to rise and inched her toes up to the very edge.

Flames licked at a log, and Brook breathed in the smell. She liked the scent of woodsmoke, she decided. Much better than trash burning in empty lots, cigarette smoke on the fire escapes, grease fires in the kitchen. Woodsmoke was rich and sweet, almost good enough to eat. It played nice with the salty tang in the air. Except...Brook wrinkled her nose.

"Sorry, Fox. That smell—I think it's my feet."

"Uh huh." His smile was pained. "I wasn't going to say anything but..."

"Ugh." Brook grabbed for her muddy socks.

"No, don't," Fox said. "I've smelled much worse, believe me, and anyway, your feet look like they could use some air."

"Ha," Brook said. "No argument there." She paused, then held up one foot and bobbed her toes at him. "Thank you," she said in a teensy voice.

Fox laughed and her toes gave him a regal nod. Brook was happy he seemed less tense. Maybe their talk had helped. Getting all that bad stuff out of his head.

"Hey!" She narrowed her eyes. "How come you don't smell bad? I mean, honestly, you smell pretty decent." Especially for a boy, she didn't add.

Fox prodded the fire and sighed.

Brook put her head on one side.

"I was hoping it wouldn't come to this," he said. "I was hoping I could keep this one secret for myself."

"Whaaat?" Brook said, "Ha-ha-ha. For your own sake, this is one secret you'd better share, buddy, or this whole place will smell like wet feet." Inwardly, she wasn't so cheerful.

Keep *one* secret for yourself, she thought. That's funny. I bet you're holding back dozens.

"Ok, you win." Fox grinned and gave the hooked sword a twist. A flurry of sparks spun upward like glowing bugs. "There's a nice pool in one of the creeks not far from here. Not too deep, so when it catches the sun, it gets less chilly. It never really gets warm, but hey." He shrugged. "The downside is that you have to use sand for soap."

"I'm in," Brook said. "Deal. It's on."

"I'll show you tomorrow," Fox said. "You'll like it."

Their conversation died away after that. Brook wanted to ask about the mystery kid in the field. Do you think he saw us? she'd say, starting with an easy question. Eventually she'd work up to, Why did you run? Was he tracking us? And if you're nervous, why don't you carry that sword and give me the knife?

She had a feeling that conversation wouldn't go well, and Team Brook-Fox was just getting back on track. In a situation like this, sharing a joke was almost as good as sharing a knife, she guessed. Anyway, pressing for answers kept you from finding out anything at all. As an orphan, if you learned nothing else, you definitely learned that.

After they each had some jerky, Brook took a long drink from the pool. She'd draped her socks over a rock by the fire where they steamed like huge earthworms. Huge *venomous* earthworms if they were from this island. Now there was a nasty thought. Brook didn't want to put her socks back on, but the evening chill made the decision for her, creeping down her bare arms and legs like invisible centipedes. *Yikes.*

She sighed and pulled on the brittle brown socks, tugging until they stretched halfway up her calves. Bits of dry mud fell off her legs. You're filthy, she thought. And you stink. And you look ridiculous, like a cheerleader for Team Dirt.

She shot Fox a side-eye to see if he was tracking her antics.

Of course he was.

"Stop judging," she said. "They're warm, like they just came out of the dryer."

He raised his brows and nodded.

Sitting by the blaze, she ran her fingers along her neck and pressed the hollow at the bottom of her skull. A day after her haircut, she still felt weird. At risk, like her long, glossy hair had been a good luck charm, keeping her safe. A charm she needed now more than ever.

You're still you, she thought. Without your hair, even without your name. How could you expect to feel normal? And what's normal anyway? Was your life at the Foundation normal? Of course not. Nothing that happened there was normal. There's no normal for you. You just stay alert. You pay attention. You keep yourself safe. That's it.

She gave Fox a little wave goodnight. He waved back and she curled up as close to the fire as she dared, angling her body so the heat would soak her face and legs and her arms, folded across her chest. She tilted her feet into the moss. Getting things arranged just right. It gave her a picture of herself, standing on her tiptoes in the Foundation dorm, tucking in the sheets on her top bunk, pulling the shabby blanket straight while someone hissed, "Loser! Goody two-shoes!"

She was glad Fox wasn't like that.

As she drifted off, she thought about the castle.

Maybe you've been looking for it a long time, without even knowing.

She woke up once, gasping for breath, fists clenched and feet jerking. The sounds of footsteps echoed in her head, and the dull, smoky light of the moon shone down like a bare light bulb. Her eyes darted right and left, then she realized the screams in her ears were night birds. The red-headed one was probably out there, looking for her and shrieking.

Brook pressed a hand to her heart and looked across the fire for Fox, but the shadows were deep. He didn't need the heat as much as she did. For a long minute, she watched the pitch dark spot where he slept, wishing she could see him. She pushed herself up on an elbow, thinking, Wait, did he leave? He's gone, isn't he? He sneaked away! Then she slumped back down.

No, he's right there, she told herself. And you're not going to wake him up. But maybe she wanted him awake, really, because she whispered, "It's just a dream." And she added, "No more cliffs that eat people. No more dragons. No more running, no more basements. You're safe now."

And she whispered louder than she needed to.

But Fox didn't take the bait.

Brook fell back asleep, trying not to think about how her whispers were lies.

CAN I HAVE THAT KNIFE?

AT THE FOUNDATION, ON THE RARE DAYS YOU GOT TO SLEEP IN, school holidays or weekends when the dorm was quiet, you stayed in bed as long as you could. For a few hours you could pretend the world was different. When you got up and looked in the smudgy mirror, brushing your teeth, it was a treat to see a girl who didn't have darkish swoops under her eyes. A girl who looked like she might be going somewhere nice.

Brook lay on her back, eyes half shut, thinking, Everything's so soft and cool. And no one's screaming at me to get up. She wasn't sure why she'd been allowed to sleep in and she didn't want to ruin it.

After a while she narrowed her eyes. What was wrong with the ceiling? Something tiny crawled over her wrist. Since when were there ants in the dorms? When she turned to look over the edge of her bunk, she found herself staring at moss and a smoking fire. Her left hip ached. She blinked and rubbed her eyes until the cliffs, the dragon, and the island got solid in her mind.

And Fox.

"Morning, Brook," he said from somewhere by the pool.

"Morning," she croaked in his direction. Since he wasn't messing with the fire, she sat up and scooted over to the stone ring, trying to remember why she felt so awkward. Oh, that was it. She'd woken up, stiff with terror, and started whispering in his direction. Luckily, Fox had slept through her kindergarten cry for help. Or had he? Maybe he'd heard her and was waiting to rub it in.

She groaned inwardly and looked at the fire-blackened sword, resting on a rock. Even coated with ash, it looked lethal. She sneaked a look at Fox, splashing water on his face. *If he didn't want me to touch it, he shouldn't have left it here.* She picked up the sword, hefted its hooked and deadly weight, and instantly stopped feeling silly.

Wow, she thought. This thing is for real. She wanted to give the blade a serious swing, slash it through the air, test its sharpness—but instead, she used it the way Fox did. What a waste, she thought. The hooked blade found an ember in the deep, warm ashes, then another. She prodded them to the surface, blew on them so they glowed, and dropped a scrap of bark on top. It felt like magic when the wood burst into flames.

"Nice work," Fox said behind her.

If he minded her touching the sword, he didn't show it. And how could he mind? He'd left it right beside her. If anything, it had been an invitation. Why don't you just hang onto that sword, Brook, he might say. Use it to protect yourself—or maybe you'd prefer this knife.

She almost smiled. *Yeah right.*

"Hunting, baths, firewood." Fox ticked them off on his fingers. "That's what I'm thinking we should do today. What do you want to tackle first?"

What about sitting by the fire and waking up? Brook thought. Or maybe you could step away for a few minutes so I can play with this very real sword.

When she didn't reply, Fox smiled. "No rush." He ran a hand

through his tousled copper hair. "You don't sleep very well, do you? I think if I remembered my own past, I'd be up half the night too. There are some scary things in your head, Brook. Something you're running from. Something that happened to you, maybe."

She realized he was watching her.

"Something you did?" he said.

Why not come out and say it, Fox? she thought. *Hey Brook, I heard you whispering last night and it was kind of freaky.*

Fox was quiet.

Normally, she would've resented his prying. A pointed question was a weapon, leveled at your chest. But Fox had a way of asking that let you know your response was optional. His questions felt like opportunities, and Brook decided to take this one. It was ok for Fox to know a little more about her. Not everything. Not a lot. Just the right amount of little.

"I dream about foster system stuff," she said. "Mean kids, bad situations, virtually no supervision. I've been in a group home for years. Do you know what those are?"

Fox blinked and rubbed his nose. "I can guess."

"You didn't miss anything." Brook tried to smile. "Not much happened inside the Foundation worth remembering. You're supposed to live there until someone wants you, but no one does—and no one wants you at the Foundation either. You just hang out with all these other unsolvable problems. Actually, I'm kind of jealous. I wish I could forget it all like you. Then maybe I could get some sleep." She sketched half-circles under her eyes.

"I hear you." Fox gave her a kind look and she thought, There, that wasn't so bad. It was about right. Now he knows where you're coming from, but he doesn't think you're a poor little baby. Good job, girl. She felt so pleased with herself that she said:

"Hey Foxy"—since they'd just been talking about their

personal lives—"I was gonna ask—can I carry the knife?" She put a mildly hopeful expression on her face.

Fox blinked. "Oh, right, that would make sense. But the thing is, I hate carrying the sword through the woods. Gets heavy after a while, and I don't have a sheath—can't stick it in my pocket like the knife, you know—so it's always getting caught on stuff. But of course you're always welcome to borrow the knife if you want. We can kind of share it between us, ok?"

Brook smiled and blew her hair back from her face. "Cool."

Wow, she thought. He really doesn't want me to have that knife.

She wondered where he'd found it. Under a rock, up a tree? Maybe she'd find one too, but probably not, with all the kids Fox said were scavenging the island. She could volunteer to carry the sword, but that would be even more awkward. It was obvious how Fox felt. It was irritating but also hard to blame him, even though he had two weapons and she had nothing. How long had they known each other, a little over thirty-six hours?

If she was in his place, she wouldn't be eager to give a razor-sharp knife to a stranger who slept a few feet away. Without a weapon it was easier for Fox to trust her and that was good. She wanted him to trust her. She needed him to trust her. But she couldn't go on like this for too much longer.

"I vote we go hunting first," she said to break the silence.

"Perfect." Fox got up, slapping dust from his jeans. "I thought we could try the tide pools today. No reason to push our luck with rabbits yet."

Rabbits and luck, huh? Brook thought. That's all you want to say about that?

Fox had a way of smoothing things over that was kind of slippery. She'd been wondering if he'd mention them running from the kid yesterday. Apparently not—but surely she'd be able to bring it up at some point. Until then, she'd be sweet and agreeable.

"Tide pools," she said. "That means fish, right?"

"Or shellfish," Fox said. "Or starfish—but only if we're desperate. They're mushy." He made a face.

"No thanks," Brook said. "I don't care for mushy—but I hope I like seafood. I don't think I've ever had it. Unless, maybe that was another memory that got zapped." She half-closed her eyes like she was trying to remember.

"Yeah, probably." Fox nodded. "They took your name and your seafood history. Makes total sense."

"Don't joke around." Brook shook a fist. "It's a crippling loss."

"It's a big deal," Fox agreed.

"If I start puking everywhere, I'll try to point myself away from you," Brook said.

"Hey, I appreciate it."

She wrinkled her nose. "No guarantees though."

He smiled like he thought she was funny.

SECRET IN THE DUNES

THEIR GOOD VIBES LASTED ABOUT A MILE.

After Brook rinsed out her mouth and took a drink, there was nothing else to do to get ready for the day, so they started walking. Their silence felt friendly, she decided. So for a while, she tried to think of what she might find that she could use as a toothbrush. Or a hair brush. They kind of overlapped. Even though her hair was short, it kept getting tangled.

As hard as she tried, she couldn't think of a single thing—except a hedgehog. She pictured herself holding one by its tiny feet and running its prickles through her hair. *Great idea, Brook. What could possibly go wrong?* But if she happened to find a hedgehog crawling around, she'd grab that cute little hairbrush.

For another couple minutes, she thought about how she was calling herself Brook and how strange it was to have no real name, just a dull spot in her mind that stayed empty no matter what. Every time she began the sentence, Hi, my name is…she expected she'd be able to finish it. But she never could.

Brook *could* be your name, she thought. It's not bad. Brooks are cool and clear. You could do a lot worse. About that time she realized the *friendly silence* had stretched into a kind of long silence as she tailed Fox through the woods, sliding through underbrush and dodging thickets. Any second now he'd say–

"What's on your mind, Brook?"

She smiled. He was getting predictable. "Do you keep track of how far you walk?" she asked. It was one of a few questions she'd stored away for moments like this.

"Hmm." Fox glanced over his shoulder. "Sometimes, but it's always approximate. I remember something about a seven minute mile–"

"That's running," Brook said before she could stop herself.

"Right," Fox said. "So I figure a hiking mile is about fifteen minutes, and that's how I figure distances."

"Smart," she said. "You just glance at your watch, or maybe your phone, and crunch the numbers."

"Exactly. I have several phones to choose from, actually."

"Of course," Brook said. "I left all *my* phones in our secret campsite, but guess I know how long ten minutes is. We're close to that now."

"Agreed," Fox said. "And heading toward the coast like we are, five more minutes will put us in the open."

"One mile to the ocean, neat and tidy," Brook said.

That's how she knew they'd walked a mile when it happened.

They'd left the woods, struggling through a prickly hedge as the sky bloomed indigo overhead, and Brook got more scratches, fighting the thorns. It was like they wanted to rip her clothes right off her.

"Fox, seriously!" she said.

"Sorry, the sea roses are everywhere. They love the coast."

She came *this* close to saying it was really too bad they didn't have something sharp, something with a long blade they could use to clear a path—you know, kind of like a machete. By the time they got out, Brook was irritable, rubbing her arms and sucking a pricked finger. Leaving the trees felt like an escape, which was weird, because diving into them felt the same way. The island made you feel like you were always looking for someplace safer, but once you got there, you realized you'd only put yourself in a different kind of danger.

"This is the south side of the island," Fox said.

"Cool," Brook said grudgingly. It *was* new information.

Her spirits began to lift as the dirt gave way to sand and grass. She saw something wide and glittering, stretched between dunes at the bottom of the sky. Her heart gave a little jump. For a second, she saw a small version of herself running and splashing through the waves.

The salty air grew even saltier, and Brook realized the sounds of the island had changed in just a few steps from the muffled, hidden sounds of the forest to a low bass rumble from the sea that crawled into your ears before you realized you were hearing it. The curve of a dune hid the ocean as they climbed, sliding in the white-brown sand, gulping breaths of tangy air. Big white gulls screamed overhead.

Brook felt excited and she couldn't help it. Wind flipped her hair around her face as they reached the top. The ocean crashed on a sandy beach a hundred feet away, and the waves rumbled even louder, like her eyes had turned up the volume. She wanted to run across the sand, kick off her shoes, and skip through the foam like that little girl.

The ocean's pull was so strong, she started to wriggle her toes in her flimsy shoes. She didn't know anything was wrong until Fox's whole body tightened. His arms flew out on either side like turnstiles to keep her from surging past. "Brook, wait!"

She felt confused as she stumbled against his elbow. Embarrassment washed the smile off her face. Why had Fox stopped her? What was wrong with pretending for just a few minutes that–

"Oh no!" Her hands flew to her mouth as she looked down

the slope of the dune. In a small valley by the cold ashes of a fire lay a boy.

Brook went as tense as a coiled spring. No one moved. The boy in the sand was even more still than her and Fox.

"C'mon," Fox finally said. "We'd better take a look."

He stalked down the dune and into the hollow, and she followed, sliding in the sand, ready to fight or run. The wind died away as the hills rose over their heads and they came to a stop.

He must be dead, Brook thought. No one rests like that. Not even if they're hurt.

The side of boy's face was pressed to the sand, mouth half open. Legs bent, like he'd been sitting and had toppled over. Or maybe he'd tried to pull his legs to his chest for warmth.

They hovered over him, keeping their distance.

Not much blood, Brook thought. You expect a dying person to bleed a lot. But arrows don't slash you open I guess.

The arrow stuck out from between his shoulders, three feet long. The shaft was thin and straight. Tufted feathers lined the end. The whole scene was strange to look at. Weird, like the arrow and the death were not connected. The arrow could've been part of a costume for a middle school play, Pocahontas or something. Instead, it had killed him.

It was hard to believe arrows still killed people.

"It was a good shot," Fox said. "I'd say it got his heart. Look at the sand, no signs of struggle. When he got hit, he just fell over."

And died, Brook thought. Died here on the beach, alone.

She looked at the sand and saw what Fox meant. She also noticed the tiny grains of sand on the kid's skin from where he'd pressed his face to the ground, taking his last breaths. She looked away.

"Someone picked him off," Fox said. "Someone ruthless."

The boy's eyes were open—at least the one she could see. His eye was greenish, the pupil rolled to one side, looking toward the dunes from three inches away. The color was close to her own eyes, a hue between brown and green, something she hadn't thought about for days. But all the boy could see was sand. Empty sand, the last thing as he died.

"Someone has a real hunting bow and arrows," Fox said. "And this person can shoot." He paused. "A sniper."

"Yeah." Brook hugged herself, caught herself doing it and stopped. "Not much of a fight."

"It was murder," Fox said.

Instantly she thought of the knife, wrapped in dirty cloth in Fox's pocket. Not much good against a bow and arrows, but razor sharp and deadly nonetheless.

He was thinking about it right now too, she was sure.

She wished it was in her pocket.

DEAD THINGS

WITHOUT PLANNING TO, BROOK SAT DOWN. SHE FELT AS IF something wonderful had been held out to her and yanked away. The sun, the sand, the big blue ocean. A few minutes splashing in the surf. She felt her shoulders tremble and bit her lip.

Death had ambushed her.

Fox looked over. Then he did something Brook never allowed anyone to do, ever.

He took her hand.

Her body stiffened like razor wire. With an effort, she made herself relax. Fox is your friend, sort of, she thought.

"Let's go," he said.

She let him tug her up the sandy hill. At the top, Brook scanned the shoreline and turned to search the field behind them. Nothing broke the flat, bright sand. If anyone was watching, he'd be a quarter mile back in the sea roses, or flat on his stomach in the waving grass. But she didn't have the feeling anyone was there.

Fox led her up a dune and down, between more hills, along a rocky string of tide pools near the glittering, angry sea. Waves pounded the beach in a battle that would never end. The same waves waited under the hungry cliffs. They didn't seem bright and lovely anymore.

"This is where I usually fish." Fox tugged her toward a little pool. The one he'd chosen was surrounded by sea-smoothed rocks. "Why don't you wait here? Check out the water if you want. I'll be right back."

She sat down on a boulder as Fox disappeared.

He's leaving, she thought. He won't come back. But she managed to stop her thoughts from running away. You already knew this was a terrible place, she thought. Lots of kids have died here—kids died the night you arrived. Gone in seconds, falling into the sea. And people die all the time. You just happened to find this body—and there wasn't a lot of blood. You can be happy about that. The kid died fast, and you didn't know him. Maybe he was a bad person. There are plenty of those.

The waves on the beach glittered. She realized the island was smirking at her again.

Surprise, surprise, it was saying. *I'll always get the jump on you.*

Brook turned away from the relentless surf. "You're still alive," she told herself. "So act like it."

She looked into the tide pool at her feet. The shallow water was colorful like a science poster. Thick grass waved on the bottom. Seaweed swirled like streamers. Tiny fish darted around like slivers of glass. She spotted a spiky brown fish, lurking by a rock. And aha!—a crab, a pretty big one, if she had to guess. She pulled her feet back from the edge, and noticed one of her big toes sticking out through battered canvas.

Great. Now her feet were crab bait—of course they were.

By the time Fox came back, she'd picked up a piece of driftwood and was herding the crab toward the shore. It kept waving its reddish pincers at her, snapping them open and shut. Neither of them had the upper hand.

"Where did you go?" she asked Fox.

He looked at her across the pool and she forced herself to keep her chin up.

"I needed a closer look." Fox held up a tangle of twine and a thin piece of metal, bent into a hook. "He didn't have much in his pockets. Maybe someone went through them." He paused and went on. "His shoes are in good shape if you're interested." He held them up, swinging from their laces.

Brook shook her head and Fox shrugged.

"I think they might fit you. Maybe he'd be happy someone had them."

"Who was he?" Brook asked. "Did you know him?"

"Never seen him before." Fox pulled off his own hikers and sat down by the pool. For a second she thought he'd try on the dead kid's shoes, but instead he stuck his toes in the water. "It's hard to keep track of who's on the island," he said. "Like I told you, a lot of these kids have gone feral. It's a mistake to get close to them—they're not even close with each other." He nodded back the way they'd come. "I guess you can see why."

Brook wanted to say, Why couldn't we all work together? But she'd lived in the Foundation. That wasn't how things went. People were always clumping into groups like paper clips stuck to a magnet. And if you weren't magnetized, and you weren't the magnet, well, it didn't matter how hard you tried to get along. You'd better watch your back. She'd learned that lesson and apparently Fox had too.

When she looked back into the pool, the crab had snuck away. She liked the feisty little thing. She was glad they wouldn't eat it.

Fox waded in, sea grass swirling under his feet.

"It's like *Lord of the Flies*," Brook said. She'd acted like she didn't know the story, and Fox probably remembered but she didn't care. "This is worse, though," she said. "Those kids kind of wind themselves up slowly, all the way to murder. It takes the entire book."

Heartless, she thought. Like Monique at the Foundation— but less headstrong than Monique, less wild-eyed and crazy. The bad kids here are more calculating.

"Here's what you've got to remember." The knife shone in Fox's hand, and Brook wondered if he wished he'd brought the sword. "Some of these kids, they've been here for an entire book. They're ready for the last chapter. They've figured out whatever they're gonna figure out and some of them are monsters. Take those blue-faces in the castle." He slashed the knife along an underwater rock, shaking his head, and Brook felt a stab of cold anger.

The blue-faces. Losers. Killers.

"Do you think they did this?" she asked.

Fox tossed a handful of lumpy black rocks to shore. "Hard to say. Normally they never leave the castle–"

"–because they don't have to," she said. "They have every-thing and they don't share."

"But you never know," Fox finished.

More rocks thudded into the sand at her feet. Why was he throwing rocks at her? Bending over, she realized they were rough oval shells crusted with tiny plants.

"Mussels," Fox said. "They take some getting used to but they're better than starfish, believe me—hey look, a crab."

Brook winced as the knife flashed down. She hoped Fox would miss but he didn't. The knife came back up with the crab on its tip, waving its legs and snapping its pincers. Fox stayed out of reach as its movements slowed.

Brook looked away and swallowed hard.

"There's something I don't understand," she said, forcing herself to think about something beside the tough little crea-ture. "Where do these weapons come from?"

Fox stepped out of the pool. "You're smart, Brook. That's

why you notice these things. Which means you probably know what I'm going to say."

Brook thought, Yeah, and you're smart too. Maybe too smart.

"Let me guess," she said, "you don't know, because where did the dragon come from? Why is there an island?"

"You got it." He dropped the crab in the sand to let it finish dying.

Brook waited to see if he'd give her one of his Fox monologues. He must have ideas or suspicions, no matter how crazy. But he didn't continue, so she carried on herself, looking away from the crab, which was making sad, jerky motions with its claws.

"This isn't an accident," she said. "We were brought to this place with monsters and a castle and weapons. Someone planned for this. Someone wants this place to be horrible. A dragon's island, littered with all kinds of nasty things..."

Brook trailed off. The crab had stopped moving.

"I hate them," Fox said, and her shoulders jerked at the anger in his voice. "Whoever's in charge," he said. "Whoever they are, I hate them."

When she looked up, his face was scary.

"Me too," she said. "I hate them so, *so* much." All the worst words she knew flew through her mind, but instead she said, "I hate those—killers." And she meant it, deep in her bones.

They collected the mussels. Brook stuffed hers in her pockets. Fox carried the dead crab. They'd reached the first dune on the trail home when Brook slowed and stopped. Her bruised toes were poking through her shoes. She sighed.

"Go ahead," Fox said. "It just makes sense."

The dead boy's shoes waited by the pool. Suede uppers. Rubber soles, almost as nice as Fox's. She didn't put them on but she took them. Dangling from springy laces, they bumped her leg as she walked. The crab looked like a wilted, spidery plant in

Fox's hand. Both of them were carrying dead things—things she wished they didn't have.

Without warning, a sob rose in her chest and she fought it down, hoping Fox wouldn't notice. She took her time catching him, waiting for her face to stop scrunching up, working to get her breathing back.

Calm down, Brook. Stop being silly. It's just a crab.

It's just a boy.

HIDDEN LITTLE WORLD

FOX HAD COVERED THE BODY WITH SAND, BROOK NOTICED. IT wouldn't stop a determined animal. Definitely not a pack of Death Dogs, based on what he'd said. But with the sand covering the scent, maybe the dogs wouldn't nose the body out. Fox had probably done it to make her feel better. She suspected that if he'd been alone, he would've left the dead kid lying where he found him after he'd gone through his pockets.

They moved fast. Fox was on high alert as they crossed the open ground, and Brook kept her head up, glancing right and left. She knew what Fox was thinking. The bow and arrows were still out there, and if someone wanted to shoot them, he could do it from a distance. Luckily there weren't a lot of hiding places in the dunes. And if the sniper was flat on his face, hugging the sand, he wouldn't be able to get a shot off.

As they left the high grass, Brook didn't see a thing. Not even a footprint. Of course, the wind had probably scrubbed those away. Then, finally, they reached the trees, and Fox started hacking at the sea roses, clearing the worst of them with the knife.

Brook didn't have the energy to be mad that he felt sorry for her. As they entered the woods, she slung the dead boy's shoes over one shoulder. They bumped her spine as she walked. They kicked her in the ribs when she shoved branches out of the way. The wet mussels in her pockets scraped her hips, making her gashed one hurt. *What I wouldn't give for a backpack.*

She didn't say anything as they hiked, and for once, Fox didn't either. Brook kept seeing the dead kid's greenish eye, staring at a floor of sand. She couldn't describe him, except for that one eye. She couldn't say how tall he'd been, or what color his hair was, or whether he was older or younger than her or about the same.

You don't know he was a good kid, she reminded herself. Not many are, and...

She tried to slow her thoughts but they ran on ahead.

...he could've died in lots worse ways.

Here she fought hard to stop, but failed.

He could've died slowly, she thought—stop it, Brook! Could've been attacked by animals or fallen off a cliff or—Get a grip!—he could've been cut, blood splashing all over, more and more until his life leaked out, gush-gush, drip-drip...dead.

Her mind stopped racing. Way too late, of course.

Talking to Fox would've been better than letting her thoughts run wild. They trudged into the boulders, down the narrow zig-zag passage to their camp. Brook dropped the shoes on her side of the fire and dug for the mussels wedged in her pockets. It felt like an ugly dance. Getting them out, she scraped a knuckle red and got black dirt under her nails. She couldn't remember ever feeling so dirty.

"Do you still want a bath?" Fox said.

How did he do that?

Brook realized she'd been staring at her dirty hands like they were objects of horror. She probably looked a little crazy. "Yes I do," she said. "I really do."

Fox nodded in a way that said, Thank goodness.

"Let's leave the mussels in the pool," he said. "I'll show you the way."

A couple minutes later, Brook hovered by the dead boy's shoes. She already knew what she would do, but she had to work herself up to it. The shoes were nicer than any she'd ever owned. Probably designed for the outdoors. She sighed, picked them up, and slung them over her shoulder again. She'd made the choice.

"Let's go," she said.

They started off through the woods in a direction she didn't think they'd tried.

"The creek runs across the forest north to south," Fox said. "We're heading west to intercept it. Not too far, and I've never seen anyone else here. It's our personal water source. One more reason to live in the trees."

"Absolutely," Brook said. "Our private creek club." She wasn't quite sure how the bath was going to work, but she had to try it. Anything to get clean. Anything up to a point.

"You're paying attention, right?" Fox said.

Brook nodded. Always, she thought.

"If you're ok with it, I'll leave you at the water and you can find your own way back," he said. "Don't worry about a trail—there's not one—but I think you'll be able to figure it out."

"Perfect," Brook said, and she meant it. If not for the dead boy, she might have actually cheered. Being alone meant she could relax, just for a little, and not have to worry about weirdness. She'd already picked out a few landmarks: rock formations, older trees, a stretch of boggy ground. It wouldn't be hard to find her way.

The woods ran downhill and the trees ahead grew thicker until Brook realized she was seeing the leafy outline of a stream. It was like seeing a rich person's lawn in summer, right next to a scraggly, brown one. The happy trees and shrubs hid the creek from the woods—like a green shower curtain, she decided.

"Push through the trees," Fox said. "Right ahead is a shallow sandy spot. Stay as long as you like. I'll see you back at camp, ok?"

"Thanks, Fox."

He nodded. Then he turned and hiked away, right on cue. Brook stood there enjoying the feeling of being alone. In the silence, she heard running water. No leaves rustled. Not a single twig snapped. She felt slightly embarrassed when she stepped behind a tree and waited for another couple minutes, just in case.

You can't be too careful, she thought.

Fox did not reappear.

See, you can trust him. At least about this...

She straightened her shoulders, blew hair out of her face, and pushed her way through the greenery. The creek bubbled over sand and gravel at the bottom of a smooth dirt bank. A few funny-looking, skinny insects skated on the surface. Other than that, she was alone. Alone—with clean, fresh water. Sun poured down on her from a patch of blue sky.

Safe. Quiet. In a place that was just hers.

Brook wished she could save the moment forever.

Then she realized something else:

"It's a brook," Brook said.

Seeing the thing she'd named herself after, and seeing how pretty it was, made her feel better than she'd felt since—well, since she could remember. She stood there awhile longer, feeling the sun on her face and taking in the magic.

It's not a bad name, she thought.

Then she kicked off her demolished canvas shoes. Threads and chunks of fabric hung off them, rubber soles sagging. The laces were shredded and covered in burrs. If she'd taken them to shop class and attacked them with a hammer and then carried them to lab and poured acid on them, she couldn't have made them worse.

Brook set the suede trail shoes beside her evil-looking sneakers. A second later, she picked the new shoes up and moved them further away—in case her old ones got any ideas. She pulled off her socks and stuck one foot in the stream. The current tugged brown wisps of dirt from her toes. Fox was right. The water wasn't bad. Not warm but not cold either. In the sunlight, it was refreshingly chilly. And who was she kidding? If it had floating chunks of ice, she'd still jump in.

She pulled the rest of her clothes off quickly and debated what to do with them. Her jean shorts were in the best condition. Thank God she hadn't been wearing gym shorts or something soft and knit. The forest would've scrubbed them off already. Her t-shirt was in sad shape, pre-shrunk cotton getting more ragged all the time. At least it was black and not sleeveless.

She folded her shorts on the bank—they were the least likely to dry fast—and clutched everything else to her chest as she stepped into the stream.

"Oh gosh, you're filthy," she said as dirt swirled off her legs.

Splashing water on herself in handfuls wasn't going to get it done, so she chose a sunny spot, took a quick breath, and sank in up to her neck. Sitting there was not bad at all. The current did its best to wash away the dirt, but the water turned clear again in moments, and her skin had never been this shade of brown, even in summer.

"That's just the top layer," Brook said. "What I need are some fish who like eating dirt." Except fish nibbling her was a gross idea. Luckily, nothing seemed interested in taking bites. The thin water bugs kept their distance and nothing else moved—except, as she was scrubbing her socks with sand, a small, brown lobster-looking thing crawled under a big stone.

"Keep your claws to yourself and we're good," Brook said.

Without warning, she found her shoulders shaking. She saw the crab, dying in the sand. She tried to make herself stop, gulping down big breaths and holding them in, but it didn't work. The sorrow kept bubbling in her lungs and throat. She put her face in her hands and let it all out.

The crab, the boy, the kids on the cliffs. Such a horrible place. And the Children's Foundation, another horrible place when it could've been so different. Sometimes she'd wanted to run around flicking ears and ball caps, saying, "Wake up! We don't have to treat each other this way. We could make things different. We could change it ourselves." But it never would've worked. It only would've made things worse.

"You've got to play the game in front of you," she said, and wiped her eyes.

She'd stopped cleaning up while she'd raised the water level with all those tears. Now she splashed cold water on her face, took a deep breath and got back to it.

After she'd scrubbed her socks and, very carefully, her shirt, she stepped out of the creek and dripped over to the trees to hang her clothes on branches. Then she splashed back in to scrub herself.

It took quite a while.

She was glad the creek felt like a hidden little world. Being naked was bad enough, and if she could've seen the whole forest rolling away, heavy with shadows, or even worse, the open, blazing plains—well, she would've had to just stay dirty. Instead, she sagged on the speckled gravel until the water touched her chin.

"How am I going to get in the castle?" she said.

She didn't know. But the next question that came to her, she knew the answer.

"Should I try to wash my hair?" she said. "Yes, I've gotta try."

It wasn't easy, using wet sand for shampoo. Combing sand through her locks with her fingers, she caught a memory of her own face, focused and serious, brushing her long brown hair in a cracked Foundation mirror. Then a hand smacked her reflection and someone sneered, "Watch out, shampoo princess."

Brook dunked her head to rinse.

After that, she spent some time with her eyes closed underwater, scrubbing her teeth with her index finger between coming up for breaths. She almost made herself laugh. By the time the bath was over, her skin tingled in a nice way except for the gash above her hip, still tender, and her scraped arms and legs, and a couple spots she'd rubbed too hard with sand.

One thing had become very obvious as she'd sat there with nothing between her heart and lungs and guts and the island but softly rushing water.

"I need a weapon," she said. "Without one I'm naked all the time."

She'd take the knife from Fox. No more playing cute.

No more messing around.

THE ON AND OFF SWITCH

BROOK HADN'T TRIED TO KEEP TRACK OF TIME. ACTUALLY, SHE'D tried not to. Fox had said to take as long as she wanted and that's exactly what she did. No one yelled at her to get out of the shower. No one said, "Stop hogging water or I'll shut it off!" Of course the water wasn't hot, but she didn't mind.

By the time she stepped out of the stream a second time, the sun had swung across the sky and its rays had less heat. She shivered, hugged herself, and flicked water off her fingers so she could pick up her clothes.

Yes, they were dry! She gave a little cheer and stood there, realizing she was not. *Brilliant, Brook.* She sighed, draped her clothes back over the branches, and stood in the brightest patch of sun, swiping water off herself. She shook her head, drops flying from her hair and danced around, rubbing her arms for warmth. A few minutes later, she was damp but not dripping.

Good enough, she decided. You can dry off while you hike.

She pulled on her wrinkled clothes, enjoying the softness. Her socks were permanently stained brown, but they smelled neutral and felt good on her feet. She sat on a flat rock for a minute, looking at the two pairs of shoes on the bank. She picked up the dead kid's hikers. What if they didn't fit? The thought scared her enough that she stopped stalling. She gave the shoes a thwack to get the sand out and tried to pull one on.

Please, please, please, she thought.

Ahh, yes!

Her heel slid right in. Her toes even had some wriggle room. Fox had been right. The dead kid's shoes were a perfect fit. You couldn't have planned it better, she thought, and right away felt bad.

"Thank you, whoever you were." She pulled on the second shoe. "I hope you were a good person." She stopped. "Well, I guess I don't hope that. But whatever kind of kid you were, I'm sorry you died. I'll put these to good use, ok?"

She tied the laces snugly and walked back and forth over the gravel.

"Whoa," she said. The nicest shoes she'd ever owned had been thrift store skate shoes, and compared to the hikers, they'd been squishy slippers. Digging her treads into the dirt bank, she bounded into the trees in three big steps.

"Now my feet are invincible," she said.

She moved uphill with long steps, enjoying the traction. Maybe this is why people like camping, she thought. It wouldn't be so terrible with shoes like this, and a sleeping bag...and a towel and toothbrush and comb...and a pack to carry it all.

She paused near the top off the hilly stretch to remember how she and Fox had come. They'd pushed through a thicket on the right, but coming back, it wasn't obvious how to get back in. The army of shrubs and saplings looked like a woven security fence.

"Time for a detour." Brook hiked to the top of the rise, swiveling right and left on her heels and thinking about how good it would feel to sit by the fire as the sun went down. Her stomach felt empty, so hopefully she'd like seafood. It was nice to worry about something that didn't really matter. The thicket angled toward her, pushing her off course, but it wasn't a big deal. Once the scrub thinned out, she'd cut back to the right—let's see, that was probably south—and find the next–

Brook froze.

A huge shadow surged toward her, eating ferns and leaves. It twisted over the ground, reaching for her hungrily. She jumped away from the darkness like it was alive. Then she got hold of herself. She looked up through the branches and saw the dragon.

Its wings brushed the treetops, and its eyes were dark gashes as it tracked her through the canopy. Neck snaking out, it plunged toward her in a rush of cracking wood. Brook screamed as its jaws snapped shut, five feet away. Its breath smelled like rust. The dragon clawed and twisted, struggling to reach her. Its oil-dark body thrashed the trees as it snarled and tore free, lifting into the air on whooshing wings.

It's leaving, Brook thought. It's giving up.

But she was still frozen in place. And then–

"Don't move a muscle, sweetheart," the dragon rumbled.

"No!" Brook said. "Oh no!"

She wanted to move. She wanted to scream and run, but–

The dragon crashed into the canopy again, tearing the forest with its claws. Brook covered her face with her hands as tree trunks groaned and shattered. The dragon forced its way through layers of branches like a diver in a green-brown lake. Its massive forearms tore through trees like they were seaweed. Leaves whirled and darted like terrorized fish. The monster's jaws gaped open. Brook had never seen so many knives.

"Oh God, help," she said.

Stretching closer, the dragon tried to cup her in paws the size of manhole covers, studded with tire irons.

Her legs unlocked. She curled her toes. Something in her head clicked On.

"Let's get to know each other," the monster rumbled.

Brook screamed and went for it. Splinters needled her legs as the dragon made a grab and missed. She'd never run so fast. The hill ahead went up in flames, blazing like a furnace, but she dodged the burning trees. She flashed through gaps—blurred through the smoke like a ghost.

The whole time the dragon was after her, snatching for her like a forty foot cat.

But Brook escaped.

Twisting right and left, darting through cracks in the curtains of fire, she got away.

She won.

Fox never would've believed it.

She reached deep woods and plunged inside. She flew past the marshy ground. She circled the rock formation. By then the dragon was gone. When she crouched under a boulder, she saw it circling overhead, spitting flame and bellowing. She was glad she couldn't hear what it was saying.

Without warning, her mind flipped back to Off. Her lungs burned like they'd been scorched. Pain stabbed her hip. Her whole body started shaking. I'm stuck in a horror movie, Brook thought. I've got to get out. I've got to get out right now.

THE INNER CIRCLE

Their campsite wasn't far, but it took Brook another hour to get there. After she pulled the splinters out of her legs, she sat on the edge of a rock slab and kicked her feet. She'd known the dragon was real—it had dropped her on the cliff. It had flown over at night, breathing fire. But looking into its dark, dead eyes, watching it inch closer, hearing it talk–

Brook shuddered.

No wonder the dragon was the first thing Fox had warned her about.

Her hike turned into a stroll. She walked from the rocks to a big tree and stopped. "Don't move a muscle, sweetheart," the dragon had said. From the tree to a thicket. "Let's get to know each other." From the thicket to the maze of boulders, where she leaned her forehead against a rock.

Something that wants to eat you shouldn't be able to talk, she thought. It's horrible, horrible—but I got away. I tried to and I did. Fox doesn't even think that's possible. She pushed her hair back with both hands, brushed off her clothes, and ran into the labyrinth.

"Fox, I saw the dragon!" she yelled as she burst into their campsite.

His head snapped up. His eyes locked onto her face.

"It tried to get me," Brook said. "In the woods by the creek."

Fox jumped to his feet and glanced at the shimmering sky.

"What happened?" he said. "Did it follow you?"

"No," she said. "I got away."

She told him what had happened, sort of—as much as she could tell. As she talked, Fox got up and paced. She sat down by the fire, as close as she could get, and pulled the hooked sword over. Holding it made her feel better as she told him about the dragon's size, its eyes and teeth and claws. Fox probably already knew, but she didn't care. "Its scales shone," she said, "like oil under a car. Like a shiny shadow."

Nothing she said seemed to surprise him, but at the same time he looked ready to jump out of his skin. Finally, she told him the dragon's words. When she stopped, his shoulders sagged in relief.

"You didn't tell me it could talk." She bit the inside of her lip.

"I hoped you'd never have to know. And that's all it said, huh?"

"Yes. Just nasty threats."

He shook his head. "Brook—I don't know what to say."

"You don't have to say anything."

"I don't know what I would've done if it had got you."

"Well, you probably would've spent the next year sobbing," she said, enjoying the picture. "But it didn't get me and I'm not gonna give it another chance."

"Ha," Fox said. "Great to hear."

She didn't tell him what had really happened. She couldn't.

When the dragon lunged at her, she'd shot away with wings on her feet. The air in her lungs had turned to hope, pure hope, as she'd found a doorway through a wall of flame—and another and another. She'd outsmarted a dragon. Who knew what else was possible?

"How about dinner?" she said.

All of a sudden, she was tired of talking about the dragon.

Fox laughed. "Tell you what," he said. "Sit tight. The dragon is a big deal. You seem like you're doing ok, but dinner's on me."

Brook gave him a smile. She felt good, at least she thought she did, but she also felt used up. She wished she had a hoodie to snuggle in. And hot chocolate, the next best thing to chocolate milk. And…

"I wish I had a book," she said.

Fox didn't notice, pulling the mussels out of the pool.

A book. It was a strange thought, because books weren't safe at the Foundation. Movies were safe. Kids chattered in the common room while the movies played, and the volume was never loud, the lights never low.

Otherwise, let's say you were totally into a film, like the one with Frodo, who seemed to have real friends—but you hear all the words and it's dark, so you're paying close attention to the screen or worse, wiping your eyes—well, you'd never notice someone sneaking up behind you. But TV at the Foundation wasn't like that.

Books were different. They were dangerous. Reading was an invitation to get hurt, and Brook could only manage a few pages at a time, constantly looking over her shoulder. She'd tried *To Kill a Mockingbird* for school, but she'd had to turn it in before she finished. When she checked books out from the library, the same thing happened. *Lord of the Flies* was the exception. No one cared about the beat-up copy she'd found, so she kept it. While she'd read that one, anyone could've pranked her or stabbed her, except she'd finally found a decent hiding place.

"Hey Brook," Fox said, "can I borrow the sword?"

She stopped day-dreaming and looked up from the fire. Wow, Fox, she thought, so casual about a blade. Good for you,

you're growing. She handed the weapon over, and he used the sword to make a bed of embers. He blew on them until they flared to life. Then he went to the rock wall where he kept the jerky and came back with a flat stone. Brook felt guilty doing nothing but watching until he gave her a sideways look.

"Enjoy it while it lasts, dragon girl."

She sniffed. "I intend to."

Fox put the stone on the fire and used an empty shell to carry water from the pool and pour it into the sunken center. A minute later, when the water was steaming, he set the mussels in.

"Aah." He rubbed his hands over the fire and sat. "Now we wait."

The water bubbled, jostling the mussels up and down.

Something had been bothering Brook.

"Hey Fox."

"Yeah."

She threaded hair behind one ear. "Why do you think the dragon came after me?"

He prodded the mussels with a stick, then looked at her across the fire. "I was wondering the same thing and, well— not quite sure how to say this, Brook." He paused. "I think we're in danger. I know, I know. Go ahead and laugh if you want."

She didn't laugh.

"That dead kid on the beach today? It looked planned, not accidental. It means people are getting picked off. And the dragon chasing you—well, it doesn't usually come crashing through the trees. Put those things together and it makes me think we're in trouble. Sometimes kids die here, you know that. But the way they die, well, it's usually not so targeted. Not so on purpose. When it feels like it was planned, it's not good. What I'm trying to say is, I think there's a list, Brook. And I'm starting to think we're on it."

Her mouth felt dry. The good feelings she had from escaping the dragon floated away.

"Sorry." Fox looked down. "This was supposed to be a good dinner."

Brook watched the shellfish juddering around. "Who do you think is after us?"

"Sure you want to talk about this now?"

She nodded.

He sighed. "I think there's an inner circle. Kids who know stuff we don't know, and kill whoever the dragon wants them to in exchange for privileges. I guess the most obvious group would be–"

"The blue-faces." Brook said it like a dirty word.

They watched the water boil.

"Yeah," Fox said.

NEGOTIATIONS

"So, how do we eat these things?" Brook asked.

Fox's knife appeared in his hand. "Let me open one for you. You let it cool down, then you kind of slurp it. And a few seconds after that...we'll know if you like seafood."

"Funny," Brook said.

They'd stopped talking about the dragon and the blue-faces, and Brook was glad. They had to figure out a plan—a survival plan—and just a little bit ago, she'd felt up to the challenge. But with every minute that went by, the island seemed more deadly, and the walls of the castle seemed higher. Death Island was closing in, reaching for them with its cliffs and thorns. The dragon and the island and the blue faces, working hand in hand.

Laughing at them. *You call yourselves a team? Two stupid kids? Just you wait and see.*

Trying to kill them. Literally. Trying to murder her and Fox.

Putting them on a list.

This place just kept surprising her with horrible feelings.

"Come on, Brook. Try one." Fox held an open mussel, revealing its creamy insides. "Only chew it if you like the flavor."

Their eyes met. Fox looked worried.

"Right," Brook said. "Thanks."

She tugged at the mussel—what was it, exactly?—and it came loose from its shell, wet and squishy. She tossed it in her mouth and chewed. Then she swallowed.

Fox raised his eyebrows. Whatever she'd seen on his face was gone.

"I think—I think it's delicious food from the ocean. And I think next time, I won't chew so much." She forced herself to smile.

It was tough to focus on the little bags of guts or whatever they were. She ate all hers because she was hungry, but she still couldn't say if she liked seafood. A little later, Fox handed her a crab leg. He insisted that she stay by the fire like she was a hero who needed to take it easy.

It was sweet of him, so she played along. But the crab made her mind flick back to the beginning of the horrible day. The beach, the boy—then the creek, the dragon. And now this. But the crab had died to give them dinner, so why waste it?

The white meat tasted tangy. Like the sea. Then all the food was gone and they were sitting back, rubbing their stomachs by the fire. Fox must be thinking the same thing I am, Brook decided. He has to be. Right? She wondered who was going to bring it up, her or Fox. She hoped it would be him. That would make things easier. Because even after the dragon's attack, she remembered the clear water of the creek—no, the brook. Her skin still smelled clean, scrubbed with sand and dried by sunshine. She wouldn't forget what she'd decided about the knife.

"You didn't throw up," Fox pointed out.

"I did not!" Brook said. "Guess I like seafood."

"That's a relief," he said. "Gotta admit, I was worried I'd have to scrub mussels out of my hair." He cleared his throat. Brook held her breath, but all he did was take the sword-poker and shove some embers around. Then he surprised her.

"So I've been thinking," he said. "It seems like we need to get inside the castle."

Her fingers curled in the moss. Yes yes yes, she thought. Here we go.

"Yeah," she said. "I mean, maybe…"

She wasn't sure how to read his face. Serious for sure. Hopeful, probably. Could he be nervous? Even Foxes had nerves, she guessed.

"I'm up for trying if you are," she said. That seemed about right. Keep him on track, thinking it's a good idea, but don't encourage him too much. Her heart gave a wild thump and she covered it with a hand because she didn't want Fox to know how much the castle meant to her. How badly she wanted to get in. "What have we got to lose?" she said.

Fox nodded slowly. The light had changed by now. In the shadows, his eyes reflected the fire. "Here's what I'm thinking," he said.

And he told her something about the middle of the night, and how the dragon wouldn't expect it in the darkness, and how the blue-faces had been on top so long they wouldn't see it coming. And how the front gate was suicide but there was a small back door, so–

Cool, Brook thought. Cool cool cool. You take care of all that Fox, and I'll take care of one other very important detail. We'll toss it in with all the others.

He'd stopped talking. He was prodding the fire, waiting for a reaction, but she didn't give him one. Finally, he looked her in the eye. "Well, what do you think?"

Brook's chin rested on one hand. She had the gesture planned. "I like it," she said. "It gives us a chance at winning. But here's the thing." She swallowed—not something she'd planned. "I'm not going to help you."

Fox's eyes got big.

"Not until I have a weapon." She forced the words out. "I'm not going out there without a weapon." She held her breath.

Fox's hands tightened on the sword. Then they relaxed. "Wow." He licked his lips. "Yeah, I can see how you'd feel that way, Brook. It makes total sense. Today was bad, really bad. And we have people trying to get us. Umm, how about this? What if I gave you the knife?"

Brook felt shocked. Could it have really been this easy? See, she thought. Sometimes you have to be blunt. Sometimes honesty works. Not usually—but sometimes it actually works! The knife. Wow, the knife.

"I'll think about it," she said to hide her confusion. "It's a very little knife."

Fox rubbed the back of his head. Maybe he was feeling surprised too.

Of course I'll take that knife, Brook thought. Of course I will. It's ridiculous I've had to wait so long. Well, too bad, Foxy, you finally found something you need more than an extra weapon. The castle, you gotta have it. And me, you need me! Did you think I was really gonna walk into a fight wearing nothing but pre-shrunk cotton? I hope you didn't think I'd play along. Yeah, Fox. Ok, Fox. Whatever you say, Fox. If you did, you're insane.

Her thoughts were starting to run away. She might say something biting. So instead she said, "It's a deal. I'm in."

She reached across the fire for a fist bump. And gave him what was probably a slightly crazy smile.

Fox smiled back.

MAGICAL FIRE CIRCLE

As THE SUN WENT DOWN, STREAKING THE SKY WITH A CHERRY AND lemon watercolor that ranked about nine out of ten, Brook wondered if the silence felt a little tense. Fair's fair, she thought. Hopefully Fox isn't a sore loser. We're both getting what we want. She curled up on the moss, favoring her sore hip, and remembered the dragon reaching for her. Snapping trees like matchsticks. Incinerating her footprints just a step behind.

I'm not afraid of you, she thought. But now that she'd seen it up close, she never wanted to be that close again. The dragon stays in the sky at night, Fox said. Too hard to track us. Too hard to see us through the trees.

She hoped he was right.

For once, Brook's dreams didn't wake her. She slept like a rag doll, didn't open her eyes until morning, and didn't remember her dreams—not that she needed to, since nightmares happened on the island while you were wide awake. When she woke up, flat on her back with an arm flung over her face, a heaviness descended on her right away, sinking through the trees like smog.

What is it? she thought. What's wrong? Oh, that's right. A hit list. Not just dead kids. Not just cliffs, not just a dragon. A list, with someone checking off names, and you're on it. Why? Why would someone want to?—no, don't even start. You're on Death Island. And it's not the first time someone has come after you, is it?

But wait, she thought desperately. There was something good too. There's gotta be. You figured something out. You learned something. Oooh, that's it. You beat the dragon. You thought you could and you did. You ran, you jumped, you dodged. And today you get a knife, a wonderful knife. So the world's not over yet. Plus, you're still clean.

Sure, she smelled like woodsmoke, but that was as good as perfume out here.

Brook sat up, rubbed her neck and arched her back. For the first time, Fox wasn't around. She went to the pool, then back to the fire, hoping to see the knife waiting—maybe with a bow on top—but it wasn't there. Well, she'd get it soon.

She sat down by the fire and started to search for embers, prodding and digging with the long black sword. When she scooted closer, her knee knocked the handle, and the sword slid into the smoking ash…and kept sliding, until half the blade was underground, vanished like a weird illusion.

"What the heck." Brook stared.

It's like a magical portal to another dimension, she thought. No, let's be real, really soft dirt. But then her imagination kicked in. *Hey. Wait. What if it is magic? What if there's hidden magic twisting through this place, watching, just out of sight. It might be the only way the island makes sense, with the dragon and the blue-faces and the castle. And if there is magic, and it opened a door and brought you here…could it have brought you for a not-bad reason?*

The idea was ridiculous and sweet, like the smell of flowers in an icy urban winter. It took her breath away. If magic brought you to a horrible place, but did it for a good reason—the magic wouldn't *have* to be bad. Right? It could be shaking its fist at the badness. Giving it the finger. Maybe good magic was invading, fighting the evil of the island. Maybe it was hanging around, waiting...for just the right person to help.

Someone who would say, Ok, I'll be the hero in this story. I'll take on the bad even though it'll make me a target. I'll do what it takes to set things right. Here I am, choose me.

Brook pictured a portal shimmering in the air, leading to the place she was supposed to be. A castle wall dissolving as she stepped onto secret stairs. Or maybe the magic reached further, spiraling away through time and space, across the sea. A doorway would sparkle and fizz into existence and she'd arrive...someplace the opposite of the Foundation, the opposite of here—somewhere open and fresh, clean and free.

Someplace magical.

A few minutes later Brook was still sitting by the cold fire, staring at nothing. She gave her head a shake. *I can't just sit here. But I'd better be careful.* She got her legs under her, ready to jump away if something flared or *whooshed*, and she took the sword in both hands. Holding her breath, she moved it in a slow circle, and...

Clunk. The blade hit something. *Thunk,* it hit something else. The sword slithered around, bumping into stuff like she was stirring a big pot of dirt stew. Dust rose in wisps and floated toward Brook's face.

Nothing magical happened. At all.

The fire ring was a dirty old fire *pit.*

"Crap," Brook said. "Well, magic could still be out there, I guess." She sighed.

The ash-filled pit was interesting, but not compared to magic. If she had a shovel and she was bored, she might dig around. Who knew what could be down there? But the air was chilly and she wanted to get warm.

Then her mind made another sideways lurch. What if Fox had buried something? She touched a finger to her chin. *Now there's an idea. You know he loves secrets. What if he hid something like, hmm...treasure—yeah, buried treasure—and he dug it out of the sand and brought it here and put it back in the ground. And naturally, the treasure belongs to the dragon, and that's why the dragon is after us.*

Brook sighed. It wasn't very convincing. Anyway, Fox wouldn't care about gold and gems. No, Fox's treasure would be a survival pack, with a pot and utensils, a few more knives, string, hooks, a compass, all that boy scout stuff. But if he had it, he'd be using it. He wouldn't have stashed it in the dirt.

She shivered and rubbed her cold arms. "Idiot."

Brook pulled the sword free and started combing for embers. Maybe she'd dig around later when the ashes were cold, although they never really were. Fox kept them hot. You didn't want to be caught without a fire. She got some twigs smoking and was looking for larger branches when he tramped in, holding an armful of logs.

"Never got our firewood yesterday," he said.

"I'll get some too." Brook jumped to her feet and wove through the labyrinth. Helping with firewood was the least she could do after that seafood dinner. A few minutes later they had a nice blaze going. Brook warmed her hands, trying not to think about magic or treasure.

Fox handed her a piece of jerky.

"We need to go back to the rabbits, Brook."

"Oh—ok." So they weren't going to talk about the castle.

"We need more food. The Death Dogs are probably gone."

"Makes sense," she said, thinking, *Give me the knife already!*

She didn't have to wait much longer. After Fox had eaten his jerky, he banked the fire and picked up the sword. He spent a few minutes wiping it down with moss. "I'm taking your advice, taking better care of this thing," he said.

Stalling is what you're doing, Brook thought. She couldn't think of anything to say so she raised her eyebrows, and then–

"Here you go." Fox handed her the knife.

Oh wow. Where had it come from? Yay! She wanted to cheer, wave her hands in the air. Instead she said, "Cool, thanks Fox."

But her heart was racing, her brain screaming: *Now you've got a chance!* She wrapped the bright blade tenderly in its dirty cloth and slid it in her pocket. *No sudden movements. No tripping.*

Patting the metal at her hip, she wondered where Fox had found it. The dragon probably didn't drop weapons from the sky. Why would it arm its prisoners? So the knife and the sword and the bow that killed that kid had probably been here all along, like tokens on a game board. If there were other weapons out there, they were already taken. Well...taken until someone died.

Died. Oh no. That meant the murderers, the blue-faces and maybe the dragon, were collecting weapons.

God, what an awful thought. The killers have a weapons stash.

Why did she always follow these rabbit trails?

"Rabbits, Brook?" Fox stood at the exit, sword on one shoulder.

Her shoulders jerked. "How did you know I—Oh."

"You don't have to come if you don't want to," he said. "You can take it easy after yesterday."

"Are you kidding?" She got to her feet. "Of course I'm coming."

Hopefully for the last time, she thought. Hunt for rabbits, out in the open?

Not fun.

Get left in the woods, alone with my thoughts?

Not a chance.

RACE TO THE WOODS

They stopped at the forest's edge and looked out over the grass. Brook shaded her eyes against the brightness. She didn't see a thing—but when did she ever? Around here, you never saw anything until it was too late.

She and Fox glanced at each other.

"Ready to take the field?" he said.

"Go team."

It was almost funny.

Fox set a quick pace, marching through the waist-high grass. Seedpods brushed Brook's elbows, and she glared at them. Stay off me, she thought. I'm still clean. Who knows when I'll make it back to the brook—or if I'll ever have the guts to go there again.

She remembered how mad Fox had been two days ago, resetting one empty snare after another as they followed the little paths. Right away, they had better luck. A fat rabbit dangled in the first trap, limp as a rag. Fox bent low in the rabbit run and Brook did too, even though she had nothing to do but watch him. Better to be out of sight, below the waving grass.

The second snare was sprung but empty. Fox replaced the sticks and loop of twine.

The third snare had another rabbit.

"Finally, a little luck," Fox said.

The fourth had one too.

"Jackpot," Brook said.

"This is more like it," Fox said.

The fifth and sixth were empty but the seventh was not.

"Four of them," Fox said. "Officially a great day. We'll be in jerky for a while. I'd stop now, but if there are more, we can't just leave them in the traps."

Without warning, Brook began to feel nervous. Things were going well. Too well. When things went better than they should, you knew something was about to fall apart. Also, she and Fox were getting close to the tenth snare where the Death Dogs had torn a rabbit to shreds. It wasn't a place she wanted to see again.

But they didn't get that far.

"Hey, what's that?" Brook said.

Something was moving on the plain, far off on their left.

Fox stiffened like he really was a fox, catching the scent of hunters.

They stared across the waving grasses.

"It's...another kid," Brook said.

Fox wheeled around. He pointed, sword tucked under his arm, dead rabbits dangling from his hands. "And another, coming from the south."

Insects whirred in the grass. The sun beat down. Brook's mouth felt dry.

She got the feeling the island was grinning.

"They're trying to cut us off." Fox's eyes were dark. "Stay close, Brook. It's a race to the woods." Then he was off and running, feet barely touching the ground. In the time it took her to draw a breath, he was twenty feet away.

This was serious.

With a rabbit in each fist, she took off after him, hair flying, trail shoes thudding. Back in middle school gym, she'd always run the laps—really ran—because the value of speed had been obvious to her for years. She flew after Fox, swishing through the grass. The knife in her pocket dug into her leg, and she hoped it wasn't cutting her.

Stay in your rag, she thought. Please don't hurt me.

Her breath came in gasps, her chest burned, and she knew one bad step would throw her ten or fifteen feet, scraping and bumping in the dirt. It would be the end. The other kids would catch her, and what could she do against a gang of them? Nothing good.

No, she thought. No, no, no.

The field was a blur on either side.

The wind made her eyes wet.

Branches whipped her arms and legs as she swerved blindly into the shade of the trees. Stumbling over roots, she threw her arms around a bumpy trunk to catch her balance. Bark scraped her face. The rabbits were squishy in her hands.

"Brook!" Fox called. "Keep moving."

Welts rose on her arms as she pushed away from the tree, but there was no blood spreading from her hip pocket.

"Good little knife," she whispered. "Stay where you are."

"They're close behind," Fox said.

She flinched when he took her elbow, but didn't pull away. She let him tug her forward, even though she'd got her legs back. He'd waited for her and he hadn't had to.

"Right behind you," she said. "I'm ok now."

His hand fell away. "We can lose them in the woods," he said.

"No you can't," said a shadow.

A tall, thick boy stepped into their path. "We knew you'd run this way," he said. "You're not the only one with brains." He looked at Fox, then Brook. "Once we deal with him..." He shrugged. "There aren't a lot of girls around. Maybe we'll keep you." His eyes flicked back to Fox and he raised his weapon, a wicked curved blade on the end of a staff.

Brook dug in her pocket for the knife.

"You've got this coming," the boy told Fox.

Then the stranger made a mistake. He glanced at Brook again.

She'd never thrown a weapon in her life. At the Foundation, you never let one out of your sight, let alone your hands. So when something dark flew past and the boy screamed and staggered, she froze. Had a bird attacked him?

Fox leapt forward. He kicked at the groaning stranger and bent over him.

Brook locked her fingers on the knife's hilt, wedged against her hip.

Fox picked up his dripping sword.

The boy stayed on his back, blood gushing from one leg.

Brook stared, then looked away. She flicked the switch in her head to On. On point, on alert, on guard. It's just blood, she told herself. It's what happens in a fight.

"Let's go," Fox said.

Branches snapped behind them and someone shouted, but Brook hesitated. She let go of the rabbits, straightened the knife in her pocket, and bent to grab the long, silver weapon the boy had dropped in the leaves. It felt cool and deadly in her hands.

Now it was hers.

"Brook!" Fox yelled.

She left the rabbits in the dirt and darted after him.

RUNNING THROUGH TREES

CARRYING THE BLADED STAFF, BROOK STAYED RIGHT ON FOX'S heels. The shadowy woods yawned open like a puzzle, but with her new shoes and new weapon, she knew more of the answers than ever before. Now she was dangerous. If there was magic on the island, then maybe, just maybe, it had decided to be on her side.

Slim and silver, the staff trailed over her shoulder like feather-weight death. She knew she'd never touched anything this lethal. Not here. Not in Weed, California. Not ever. If she turned and fought, she'd be scary. Even Fox would be impressed. But you never knew how a fight would end.

Fox didn't stop running and neither did she. They were moving so fast she couldn't waste a single breath. She couldn't miss a single step—and she didn't. Feet gliding, knees pumping, the staff slicing the air behind her, she stayed in rhythm.

She had the feeling she and Fox were leaving their pursuers behind. He must have sensed it too, because a few seconds ahead of her, he swerved away, off the straight line they'd been running. Brook skidded and made the turn. When Fox glanced back, he looked surprised to see her right behind him.

Then he slowed to fight through thick brush, the bristling, twisty kind of stuff they'd been avoiding. Brook shoved at vines and saplings, slashing with her staff. Fox was right, a big weapon was awkward in the forest—but the blade sure was sharp.

When she came out the far side of the thicket, leaves clinging to her clothes and hair, Fox was climbing an enormous slab of rock. She'd seen the leaning stones before. They'd run away from their campsite, cutting north through the woods toward the castle.

She scrambled up the angled rock, enjoying the way her shoes grabbed hold. Before, it had been like falling up a playground slide. Now it was an uphill jog. When she reached the top and jumped down next to Fox in the jumbled boulders, she saw why he'd brought them here. Looking back, there wasn't a trace of their escape. No scuffed leaves, no broken twigs. No footprints. Hiding behind the rocks and spying, they could watch the hillside without being seen.

Brook felt good, ready to run *or* fight.

If someone else threatened her, he'd regret it.

"Now we'll see if we've lost them." Fox set his rabbits down, then his sword, and slumped in the shade, chest rising and falling. The rabbits looked the worse for wear from being squeezed.

Brook wiped damp hair off her face, leaned against a boulder and slid a hand into her pocket. The knife was resting quietly, flat against her hip. Knowing what a razor edge like that could do, she felt grateful. She wanted to sit down like Fox, but she didn't want to set aside her bladed staff. The silver arc gleamed in the sun. It felt powerful in her hands.

Don't be silly, she told herself. No one's gonna snatch it. You're not in the Foundation. But still. She leaned it against a boulder, tugged the knife half-out of her pocket, and slid to the ground between Fox and the staff—just in case he made a grab.

"Why didn't we fight them?" she asked.

It seemed like such an obvious question.

Fox tilted his head back against the rock and closed his eyes. "They were organized," he said. "And there were probably more of them—and they had weapons."

"Yeah, but..." Brook took a big swallow of air. "We do too."

Fox opened his eyes and looked at her. His gaze slid up and down the staff.

"True," he said, not giving much away.

She could imagine what he was thinking. Woo-hoo, Brook picked up a spiky staff-thing. She's been here four days and she's never touched a staff-thing in her life. But all of a sudden she thinks we're invincible. And she left behind her rabbits.

Maybe she was making up the part about the rabbits, but Fox had managed to hold onto his. She felt her face get hot and looked away, back down the long stone slab. The slope was empty in the sun.

She had the crazy urge to jump to her feet, grab her weapon, and show Fox she wasn't just a clueless girl. But she managed to catch her breathing as it started to speed up. She smoothed a hand across the front of her shirt. *Let him be.*

She checked the slope again. Still empty.

"It's a nice scythe-staff," Fox said. "In great shape, too. I'm jealous."

"Scythe-staff, huh? Cool name." Brook knew he was being polite. He had a knack for that. Well, it wasn't a bad quality. She crooked an arm around the staff and flashed a smile. "Don't tell me you want to trade," she said.

"Wow, seriously?" Fox narrowed his eyes, thinking about it. For a scary second, she thought he was about to say, Yeah, let's swap. Then he winked. "Naw, too pretty for me."

Brook smiled again, and this time she didn't fake it. The staff was hers. She was happy they'd nailed that down. *Scythe-staff.* It sounded good.

"I'm starting to think we lost them," Fox said.

"What if we didn't?"

"We'll see them coming and sneak away. By the time they get up here, we'll be halfway down." He pointed to the other side of the ridge, where boulders tumbled down to meet the trees. "And when they get up here, no trace of us."

Brook nodded. "That's pretty genius, Fox."

He shrugged, looking a little smug.

Slumping in the shadows of the rocks, she felt her muscles getting tight. Her lungs ached. Jumping and dodging through the woods, sprinting uphill, then this. Her gashed hip was smarting. Her stomach was unhappy. She should be walking it off and stretching her city muscles at the very least.

Brook stood up, half-crouching to stay below the rocks. She took her scythe-staff—she couldn't help herself—and crept forward to the castle overlook with the rock slide at her back. Fox didn't say a word, just watched her push through the evergreens.

The cliff fell away at her feet. She planted the staff like an explorer and looked out over the green and amber plains. The castle towered in the sun, even bigger than she remembered. A monument to safety and strength. Brook took a breath so big that her shoulders lifted. There really is magic here, she thought. Something good, waiting and watching. How else can you explain that?

"Gorgeous, isn't it?" Fox said behind her.

Standing there with a hip cocked, looking over the glowing fields, leaning on her scythe-staff with a certain swagger, Brook knew the castle was the right decision. The kids trying to kill them would never expect them to go there. Together, she and Fox could get exactly what they wanted.

ISABELLA

THEY WALKED TO THEIR CAMPSITE THROUGH UNFAMILIAR WOODS. Fox would've probably liked to talk—he usually did—and Brook felt like talking too, but she also felt giddy. The scythe-staff trailed over her shoulder like a sharp, curved streamer, making her think God was real—and hey, maybe God was behind the magic. Good things could still happen. Even with all the death.

She wanted to tell Fox, but she knew it would come out crazy:

"Fox, what if we're the good guys? What if we ended up here for a reason and we don't need to be afraid? We'll take over the castle and rule like a king and queen. We'll make a civilization with our own laws. Forget *Lord of the Flies*—we'll be *Lords of the Butterflies*! And later, we'll build a boat–"

Yeah, she was glad she wasn't saying this. It was over the top all right.

It just felt so good to win.

Yesterday she'd escaped the dragon. Today, the hit-kids. *You've got us on your list, so what? Eat our dust. And watch out, losers, we're coming for your castle. You blue-faces made a mistake coming after me and Fox.*

Hmm. Thinking about it, she couldn't remember if the big, tough hit-kid in the woods had been wearing face paint. Trying to recall his face now, she wasn't sure—so many shadows. But it was obvious which side he was on.

Once she calmed down, Brook tried to get her bearings in the forest. The trees were big and twisty with bark like alligator hide. It made walking easier, since the forest giants sucked in all the light and water for themselves. No rude vines, no grabby little shrubs. The ground was thick with rotting leaves.

She got the feeling they were being watched. Once, when she looked up, something twisted across a patch of sky. Her chest tightened. But it could've been just a broken branch, moving in the wind.

Later, something howled off to the west. Fox didn't comment but he moved a little faster. They'd walked at least an hour, about four miles, when he stopped and looked around. His face darkened. Brook got the idea he wanted to cuss. Instead, he lashed out with his sword, slicing splinters off a tree. Brook's hands tightened on her staff, but a second later he was calm again.

"Back we go," he said like nothing had happened. "I got off track."

They doubled back. Brook's muscles began to stiffen up, and her good spirits started to leak out. Maybe it was her fault for staying quiet, but she felt like Fox should've been happy too. A little cheerful at least, after their big escape. It made her feel silly. Maybe she wasn't thinking straight. Maybe the future wasn't bright if Fox didn't even see it.

No, she thought. He's in a bad mood. *I'm* right. Something good *can* happen.

But it made her irritable.

After they'd hiked two miles back the way they'd come, they stopped under a huge, pale tree with swooping branches and bark peeling off in big strips. *With our luck, it's probably haunted.* Fox chose a new angle—maybe southwest, Brook thought—and they set off, escaping the ghost tree. Their direction didn't seem very different from the way they'd gone before. But this time it worked.

When they found the creek, Fox looked at her and nodded. She checked his face for signs of anger, but he seemed ok. They followed the watercourse south, and long before they passed her bath spot, Brook knew where they were. When they reached the bottom of a wooded hill with the stream bubbling at their backs, her heart rate spiked.

"Um, Fox?" She paused, probably standing in her old footprints.

"We'll stay away from the burn area," Fox said.

She wasn't even surprised when he read her mind. She must be getting used to it. But she felt very nervous, creeping through the shadows. The scorched ground opened on their left as they wound through the thicket. Wisps of smoke rose from the blackened ground. Trees were snapped and broken like forty-foot toothpicks, and it was hard to believe anyone had survived. Fox looked at her and raised his eyebrows.

She kept an eye on the sky but it stayed empty.

The dragon was looking for them somewhere else.

By the time they wound through the standing stones and into their campsite, Brook's feet ached in her new hikers. Her scratched arms and legs had started itching.

"Camp sweet camp," Fox said.

"Not quite home, is it?" she said.

"Huh?" Fox itched behind one ear.

"Never mind."

"Ok. Gotta say, I'm sick of carrying these rabbits." He dumped them by the fire.

Brook got a drink, then leaned her staff against the rock on her side of the camp. She slumped beside it, and the cool, smooth stone soothed her back. Propping her chin on one hand, she studied her weapon. Its sculpted wooden handle rested in the moss. The dark, swirly blade shone against the granite. It could've been a weapon photo shoot.

"Not many blades like that," Fox said.

She turned. "Sorry I dropped my rabbits."

"It's ok, there's always more."

She nodded, happy he was being cool. She could tell he was tense, maybe angry, but he did a good job keeping it in check. That was something she understood. She wondered what he'd think of her if he got to know her better and saw that side of her. Well, it would happen eventually. And if anyone could understand, he should.

Fox got the fire going as Brook splashed water on her arms and legs. "Want me to skin the rabbits?" she asked. "I can pitch in."

"Thanks, but it's tricky," Fox said. "How about next time?"

So she handed him the knife and watched as he sliced the rabbits open, carved away the guts and peeled away the skins. She even made herself watch when he cut the heads off.

"I figure we can eat one and make jerky with the other," Fox said.

Since they'd skipped breakfast and lunch, they ate first. Brook took a turn with the knife, slicing one rabbit into chunks on a flat rock. They roasted them over the fire, licking their lips, and ate them almost too hot to chew.

"Wow." Brook said. "So good."

Fox smiled at her and some of her hope came back. *Look at us, sharing the knife like a couple good kids on kitchen duty.* She wondered if the two of them were friends. Whoa, she thought. Slow down, Brook. Take it easy.

"Hey," she said, "Do you ever feel like your head will explode?" She'd meant to go on, but instead she stopped on a dime and shut her mouth to see what Fox would say.

He kept slicing the second rabbit into strips. "Yeah, Brook. All the time."

"Seriously?" She waited.

"There's all these threads to keep track of," Fox said, "to hold together. Eating, hunting, planning, hiding. Gotta keep them tight and lined up, but you never know when your brain will surprise you and say something like, Man, I wish I'd had a chance to play baseball—I could've been really good. You know? And then everything twists into a tangled mess and starts burning, if you let it. I think my head's exploded a hundred times."

"Thank God, you get it." Brook touched her forehead. "I mean the island, the dragon, the castle, it all just whirls around in here. Why are we here? What's the point? If I'm not thinking about something else, it's like a firestorm in my head. The harder I try to figure it out, the worse it gets."

"That's why it's a good idea to stay busy." Fox handed her a skewer. "And if the bomb goes off, oh well. Maybe brains work better on fire."

"Maybe." Brook skewered chunks of rabbit. "Although I'm not sure I want my head on fire all the time. Sometimes I try to think about smaller questions instead, like—where does the dragon go when it's not flying? Where does it sleep?"

"That's a good one." Fox paused, the knife hovering. "Maybe a cave in the cliffs that can only be reached by air?"

"Probably," Brook said. "You think we should try to find it?"

"Probably not," Fox said.

"Right," Brook said. "Why die young? But it's the kind of thing I think about."

Fox tapped his own forehead. "You and me both."

She wanted to say something about magic, one of the explosive questions tumbling around her mind. "Hey Fox, what if good magic is carving out space on the island? What if the magic brought us here? What if the magic has a plan of its own?" But if she and Fox were friends—big IF—they weren't close enough for *that* talk.

Still it made her feel good, bringing more of her thoughts into the open.

They finished cutting up the second rabbit, and Fox showed her how to build a drying rack over the fire with Y-shaped upright branches and a center stick. After they hung the meat in the smoke, they sat by the blaze as the sun went down.

As soon as it was dark enough to feel like bedtime, Brook said goodnight. It made her seem like an eight-year-old but she didn't care. The wind and sun and running had made her bone tired. Before she curled up, she touched the handle of her scythe-staff.

"The island didn't want me to have you," she whispered. "But I got you anyway."

As she lay in the moss, she tried to think of a name for her weapon. She didn't know that many. Not her own. Not Fox's. Not many names at all. Monique, but that was the last name she'd give anything she liked. Names without faces fluttered around her mind like moths. Finally she settled on Isabella. She couldn't say where she'd heard it, but the staff deserved something nice. Something graceful. Isabella didn't sound especially deadly, but to make up for that…she would name the knife too. Maybe Fox would let her keep it, and then the knife and scythe-staff could balance each other out.

Hmm.

Demon-fang?

Dragon-tooth?

She fell asleep trying to think of something nasty.

That night she dreamed again. The gang of girls were on her tail, and the chase started by the bus stop, but she ran so fast and so far that she was on the cliffs, and the dragon came straight at her, roaring and snatching with its teeth, and she screamed and fell, down into the grinding mouth of the sea. But she landed in the woods, shoving through branches that exploded into splinters. Gasping, she ran deeper in, where the trees grew old and the silence was haunted. But somehow, even though she dodged and twisted, quick as a rabbit, the chase still ended in the basement.

It was the worst nightmare she'd ever had.

She woke up, shaking, when the dragon flew overhead. The real dragon. Soaring so close she could feel the rusty bass vibration of its roar. In her dream, the roar had been a city sound, an evil subway rumbling to life, and she didn't know how it would fit into the awful things that were happening, only that it would make them worse. Maybe the train would smash through the basement wall and she'd find herself on the tracks.

Her eyes flew open and she saw crimson flames eating up the night. The dragon could've seen her if it hadn't been for the screen of branches. The beast was flying low. She figured it could see in the dark since it had dropped her on the cliffs at night. She held her breath. She could have been a mannequin, lying on its back. The dragon wheeled and came around again. Fire burned behind the leaves, turning them blood red. Maybe the dragon smelled them.

Then it gave up and flew off toward the coast.

Thank God.

Brook lay awake for a long time. She could barely bring herself to move, to wipe her forehead and unbend her cramped legs on the moss.

"Fox," she gasped.

"I saw it too." He sounded hoarse. "But everything's about to change, Brook. Remember that."

She did her best to believe him.

KILLER KIDS

THE HIT-KIDS FOUND THEM A LITTLE AFTER DAWN.

Brook came awake knowing something was wrong. Fox was on his feet in the gray light. The hooked sword was in his hands, but he hadn't touched the ashes of the fire. His head was on one side. Then she heard it too.

A rustle of leaves. Creaking branches.

It could've been the wind.

But it wasn't.

Brook jumped to her feet, ignoring her throbbing hip and aching legs. Her heart rattled her ribs—SLAM SLAM SLAM— as she snatched Isabella from the rock. In the second it took her to wheel around, a shadow had dropped into their hollow—and all her reflexes tightened to a razor point.

It's happening, she thought. They're still after us. Ok, ooh-kay.

Something flared to life in her chest and set the rest of her on fire.

The shadowy boy flicked his hand. A dagger ripped Fox's shoulder and clanged against the rocks. The boy moved closer. "Did you really think we'd let you—"

Fox didn't throw his sword this time. He yelled and threw himself.

Covering the distance, he brought his sword down in a fierce two-handed chop. Metal crashed on metal, and then the two boys were circling each other, hacking and dodging. The stranger had a gleaming spear-like thing with extra blades. Brook could hardly see it in the dark, but the kid kept using it to stop Fox's blows. She heard sounds on the path through the standing stones.

More killer kids were coming.

Go, Brook thought. Hit the switch.

She lowered her staff and ran at the shadowy boy. He saw her coming, and she didn't make it easy for him. To stop her, he'd have to turn away from Fox. Could he fight them both at once? Brook swiped with Isabella, just as quick and deadly as she'd thought. The stranger lashed out, their blades clashed, and she found her answer.

No, he couldn't fight them both. He knocked her blade away, but Fox cut at his legs and the boy went down with a scream. Fox's sword flashed again. He snatched the forked weapon from the kid's limp fingers and turned.

"Who's next?" he snarled.

More shadows spilled from the labyrinth, appearing as if by magic. One, two, three. Brook couldn't make out faces but their weapons glittered in the dawn.

Fox's arm whipped forward. The forky weapon shot through the air.

The first shadow made a choking sound and fell.

"Now it's two on two," Fox said like he was keeping score.

God, help, Brook thought. Here I go.

Fox stepped forward and she kept pace on his right. She held the scythe-staff level, hovering like a snake. The last two kids fanned out on either side. The third one lay twitching on the ground.

Fox laughed.

Then the two shadows did something Brook never expected. They split up. One went left, one right. The fight became two games of one-on-one, and Brook was ok with that, because if there was one thing she hated, it was multiple people coming at her at once.

Her attacker rushed in, closing fast with a spiky bat like Brook was a piñata, waiting to get cracked. *But I'm not.* She dodged the first swing and her attacker stumbled past. When the kid whirled, Brook realized she was fighting another girl—a girl with angry eyes and a bruise on one cheek. The girl took another swing, and Brook saw her opening. She snaked the scythe-staff under the bat and gritted her teeth when the blade hit something solid. The other girl screamed and staggered away, holding a bloody arm. Now her eyes looked wild.

That's what you get, Brook thought.

But her attacker still hadn't had enough. She pushed off from the rock wall, ready to come at Brook again—until she saw her weapon, pinned under Brook's foot. The girl's face changed and she made a dash for the labyrinth. *Go ahead and run,* Brook thought. *This isn't over.* Ahead of her, the killer bounced off a boulder, scuffled in the dirt, and made a wrong turn.

Brook smiled.

When Brook arrived at the dead end, the other girl had her back against the stone. Her face was a mask and her hands were in the air, saying Hey, don't hurt me, this was all a big mistake— but Brook knew what the killer kid would do if she lowered Isabella or looked away for even one second. The girl would jump at her, clawing and spitting like a dumpster cat.

Brook didn't give her the chance. She leveled the scythe-staff, gauged the distance, and pivoted on one foot to put her strength behind the blow.

"Don't!" The girl's hands started shaking. Her eyes widened

until they took up her whole face. "I can tell you things! There's a plan, a reward! Please, I can–"

"Liar!" Brook spat. "You came here to kill us in our sleep. You can't tell me anything that'll keep me from–"

Wait, she thought. *Is this it—the way you're gonna choose? The you you want to be?* Her whole body felt ready to plunge ahead. To cut, to stab, to end this, so she'd never have to see the girl again. Then her rage and the blood boiling behind her eyes crashed into something big and dark that flashed like lightning, and she thought, *But magic. You can't do this and have magic. Not both.* So she stepped back, never taking her eyes off the killer, who was holding up her hands like melted talons.

"Get out," Brook said through her teeth.

The girl shot past down the trail through the jumbled rocks. Cradling her bloody arm, she looked back once. Then she was gone—but still out there. Still dangerous. Half of Brook wished she'd ended the fight for good. *And the weird thing is, I don't even know if there* is *magic.* Brook's death grip on the scythe-staff weakened. "Well Isabella," she said, "at least it still makes sense for you to have that pretty name."

When she turned, Fox was coming to a stop behind her.

"Brook!" He dropped his sword and put his hands on her shoulders. "Are you ok?"

"Yeah. Are you?"

"I'm fine." He stepped back, taking her in. "Really, you're not hurt?"

"I'm great, Fox. I won."

He kept staring, probably checking for blood. Then he looked past her down the trail.

"I let her—she got away," Brook said. "But I cut her good."

"Maybe I'll show her to the door," Fox said.

And just like that he was gone.

Brook walked back to their campsite.

Standing by the fire, she caught herself breathing hard

although she'd barely done a thing. Fox had done the real work, moving from weapon to weapon and fight to fight like it was nothing. It had been a performance.

"But I could've done more," she whispered.

One killer-kid was down by the standing stones. Fox had thrown the silver fork like a huge dart, straight to the bullseye. It had hit the kid in the neck. A second killer, the boy who'd jumped into their campsite, was crumpled in the moss like he'd dropped from the sky. The third kid Fox had fought lay face down near the fire, turning the ground red. Brook didn't need a closer look. Three less killers on the island.

So that was that. Seeing them now, cluttering their campground, she was happy with what Fox had done. She wasn't sure why she hadn't done it too. There wasn't any magic here. Just survival. *Just the most deadly wins.*

Brook yanked the fork-weapon free. Blood pounded in her ears.

She realized she was furious.

"How dare you," she said.

She kicked at the ground. She stalked back and forth between the three dead bodies.

"You thought you could kill us in our sleep," she said. "And now you're dead. How do you like that? Dead, you losers, dead." She was fighting for breath again. So she leaned her staff against the granite and stuck the fork-spear in the ashes so she could go to the pool, where she took a drink and splashed water on her face and hands.

"I need a toothbrush," she said.

Her mouth tasted awful.

She stood by the fire, looking around.

"They bled all over the moss." A sob caught in her throat.

Feeling sick, she sat in a clean patch by the embers and pulled her knees to her chest, digging through the ashes with the giant fork. It worked much better than the sword. She put a hand to her stomach. Things had just started to go well.

"It's ok," she gasped. "It's ok."

She was glad Fox didn't reappear.

After a while, she straightened up, wiping her eyes and nose, rubbing her hands in the moss. Her breathing had returned to normal.

"They deserved it," she said. "We didn't have a choice."

She focused on the smoking ashes. Usually they'd have the fire going by now. Usually they'd be waking up slowly (well, at least she would) and Fox would be saying what they needed to get done that day. It took more work than usual to dig for embers. She found a few small ones on the surface and jabbed the fork-thing deeper. It snagged a glowing, fist-sized chunk.

Brook pushed hair out of her face and dug in again, looking for more lava coals. The fork connected with a solid crunch, and she tried to lever it up. It quivered in her hands and didn't budge.

"What the heck," she said through gritted teeth.

She twisted and shoved and jerked. Sweat popped out on her forehead. The ashes of the fire swirled and collapsed like the mouth of a volcano opening.

"Come—on!" Brook groaned and yanked.

The silver fork came up in a dusty cloud. Ash swirled into her eyes and nose. "Ack-blech!" She coughed, waving away the choking air. Before the dust could cover any more of her, she stumbled to the pool and splashed herself again. So much for being clean. Then she went back to the fire to see what she could salvage. Smoke rose from the dusty ruins.

Brook slid the forked weapon slowly from the ashes.

No more ash explosions, she thought. I've had enough–

"Oh God!" She dropped the weapon.

Looking up at her was a blackened, grinning skull.

WEAPONS-RICH

WHEN FOX GOT BACK, THE FIRE WAS COLD AND DEAD. BROOK SAT in her usual place, knees pulled up, arms around her shins. The skull sat next to her in the moss.

They stared at Fox, together.

"Whoa!" Fox put a hand on his heart. "That one rotted fast."

"Not funny." Brook forced herself to pat the skull. It had been sitting in the coals forever, so it had to be sterile, right? "Want to tell me about this?"

Fox came to stand by the ruined fire. Streams of ash were still trickling into the cavity Brook had opened underneath. It looked like the charred ruins of a tiny ancient city.

"Where else could I put it?" Fox said. "I didn't have a closet to hide it in."

"Why didn't you tell me about it?" Brook said.

"Why would I?" Fox crossed his arms. "Do you think I've told you about every horrible thing that's happened to me here? All kinds of things. Once I cut myself on a reef and Death Dogs smelled my blood and almost got me. Once the dragon chased me into the woods. I had to hide in the brush for days. And speaking of monsters, if you want to get really practical, do you think it's a good idea to leave a body in the forest by your camp-site? Cremation made sense."

Brook crossed her arms.

"I've been attacked before," he said. "I may have mentioned it once or twice."

She waved a hand in the air. "I guess everyone just hates you."

"If you're not part of their little gang, then yeah, they hate you," Fox said. "We've talked about this. Something tells me you might know a little about it too."

Brook closed her mouth. He'd taken the wind right out of her. Fox was right, of course he was. He was the one living in reality. She was the one struggling to keep up.

Fox leaned several weapons against the rocks. One was the silver bat with spikes Brook had taken from her attacker. There was some kind of black axe and a gleaming spear with a leaf-shaped blade. Plus Isabella, and the huge barbed fork, and the little knife she hadn't named yet. Oh, and the knife the kid had thrown at Fox.

"Did you kill the last one?" Brook asked.

Fox shrugged. "Do you want me to tell you what happened?"

"Not really," she said.

"I bought us time," Fox said. "They won't come after us for a while. But we can't stay here much longer, Brook. If they can find us once, they can find us again."

"You're right," Brook said. "And then there's the dragon. Flying over, blasting flames around like fireworks—or signal flares. 'Hey everyone, here's where Fox and Brook are hiding.'"

Something wild flickered through Fox's eyes.

Panic? Rage? She couldn't tell. Brook looked around their secret campsite. Like the fire, it felt caved in on itself. Dirty with death and ash.

"Fox, can I ask you something?" She pointed at the three bodies. "Is this easy for you?" She took a good long look at him.

There was blood on his shoulder from where the dagger had caught him. Other than that, he looked unhurt. Even relaxed.

"Is what easy for me?"

"This," Brook said. "Killing."

Fox blinked. She held her breath.

"No," he said. "It's not easy."

She waited.

"I hate this." All of a sudden, his face looked young—about her age, no older than fourteen. "I try not to think about what I'm doing," he said. "Because if I do, I'm dead." He pointed a finger at her. "And so are you. I'm a friendly guy, Brook, or I would be in normal life. I wish you could see that part of me. I'd rather be playing kickball or watching a movie or doing homework. I wish we were normal friends and we could work on a class project or walk to McDonald's. But we're not, are we?"

Brook felt bad. What did she expect from him? Definitely nothing normal.

"Sorry," she said.

Fox studied his feet. With his head down and his shoulders slumped, he looked less confident and more like a kid. Brook stepped closer. She held her breath as she put a hand on one of his shoulders and squeezed. He covered her hand with one of his. They stepped apart.

"Thanks," he said.

"I get it," Brook said.

Ash floated up the yellow sunbeams into bright green leaves. The morning was half over and they hadn't eaten and there were three dead bodies lying in the moss.

"At least we have a lot of weapons now," Brook said. She was trying to picture Fox in a McDonald's. Or playing kickball. It was tough.

"We're weapons-rich," Fox said. "Which one do you like best?"

Brook looked at the new ones he'd lined up. Strange, sharp

lines gleamed bright and deadly. The slender spear was tempting. The axe and the spiky bat—a mace, Fox said—were on the heavy side and not as sleek.

She picked up the fork-spear from the fire. It had a brutal quality that she didn't love, even though it reminded her of her old Foundation shork. Maybe that was why she didn't like it. In the end, she decided to stick with Isabella. The scythe-staff was strangely pretty. Doing its job with all the style it could.

"Good choice." Fox smiled.

"What are you so happy about?"

"It's a gorgeous weapon."

"So?"

"It's kind of girly."

"Ah, I see." Brook put her hands on her hips. "So you're happy I didn't choose one you'd actually want. In that case..." She grabbed the fork-spear. "Mine!"

"No!" Fox pretended to be shocked. "I wanted that trident."

Brook narrowed her eyes and snatched the spear. "Also mine!"

"Hey! Stop being greedy!"

Brook wanted to keep grabbing weapons but her arms were full. "Hmm. Carrying all these is going to be tricky."

Fox hoarded up all the rest, pretending to be desperate.

They looked at each other and laughed.

"Let's eat something," he said. "Then we'll deal with these bodies. Then let's talk about the castle."

KEY TO THE CASTLE

THEY STARED AT THE CORPSES. BROOK WAS PRETTY SURE THAT'S what you called dead bodies—or was it cadavers? She preferred to call them Hit-Kids One, Two and Three, but no matter what she called them, when she looked at them she felt numb.

"I'm not sure what to do," Fox admitted.

Brook nodded. All their different problems smashed together made it hard to think.

"We could burn them," Fox said. "But believe me, you don't want to be here while that's happening. So we'd have to stay away from our campsite, and it's not a great time to be out hiking. We could drag them into the woods, but they'd attract —attention."

Death Dogs, Brook thought. Vampire birds. God knows what else. She pulled her eyes away from the bodies, feeling trapped, like the kids were still threatening them, holding them hostage with their flat, cold eyes. She wanted to stop thinking about it, but the hit-kids wouldn't let her. Her chest was tight. She needed the corpses gone.

"What if we move them into the woods," she gasped. "But we take them far enough away so…"

"So whatever finds them won't find us." Fox nodded. "It might work, for a while."

Brook found a patch of blue sky and studied it. "These kids —they're more trouble dead than alive." Her mind was in such a weird place, she didn't realize it might sound funny.

When Fox laughed, she tried to smile.

In the end, they dragged the bodies through the labyrinth by their feet. Brook looked at trees, rocks, spider webs—anywhere but down. She tried to act like she was dragging bags of laundry or trash. By the time they'd pulled the third body a quarter mile, she was flushed and sweaty, dirt sticking to her skin. She thought she might be sick. But *what else can we do?* she thought. *We need them gone.*

She inspected the forest's bright green ceiling as Fox covered the corpses in dead leaves and branches. "That'll buy us some time," he said.

"Good." She hoped they wouldn't need a lot, because she didn't think she could stay in the secret camp much longer. She wiped her forehead, rubbing her dirty skin, and stopped with a hand under one eye. "Wait," she said. "What happened to their face paint?"

Fox frowned. "They must take it off when they leave the castle," he said.

"Figures." She sighed.

They walked back to the campsite.

"How are you feeling?" Fox said.

Brook knew he didn't need to ask. She slumped in a blood-free patch of shade, hunching over her jerky, which seemed extra tough. The fresh rabbit and seafood had spoiled her.

"I'm great," she said.

I'm so angry, she thought. *And I'm not even sure at who.*

"I don't know about you." Fox was inspecting their weapons. "But I think we need to move." He waved a hand around the hollow, at the caved-in fire, the splashes of blood. "We can't stay here."

Brook blew out a long breath. "Yes, I'm with you. It's not secret anymore." Or safe or pretty, she thought. Not a place I want to read a book or sleep. It's ruined.

"You ready for the castle?" Fox said, using that knack of his.

"Sure, I'm ready." Yes oh yes, her heart said. *Now is the time.* Brook thought of *her room*, high in a tower, sunlight through the window, a lock on the door. Where she could sleep or think or just do nothing. "How are we gonna take over?" she asked. "Now that we're on a list, we'll have to fight every single blue-face, won't we?"

Fox smiled. "Here's the thing. The castle has a key."

"What?" Brook stopped looking at Isabella and turned to Fox. She narrowed her eyes. "But how is that going to–"

"The key hangs in the highest tower," Fox said. "That's where it's always kept. And if someone takes the key—he rules the castle."

"That doesn't make sense."

"It's weird." Fox nodded. "But you've gotta believe me. After a while you know where the tide pools are, where the rabbits run, and you know that only the best kids make it off the cliffs. You know that weapons are incredibly hard to find." He took a deep breath. "You figure out how things work, sort of."

"Why would there be a key?" Brook said.

"Why is there an island?" Fox ran a finger over the blade of the axe.

She saw his point. Then her shoulders twitched. *What if there's a key because—magic? So good can win. So the hero has a chance?* She didn't want to believe it after what had just happened, but she couldn't keep her heart from beating faster.

"The castle isn't supposed to be locked down." Fox picked up a handful of moss. "It belongs to whoever holds the key. But when the blue-faces took over, they shut everyone else outside. No one has a fighting chance. No one can challenge them. Seems wrong, doesn't it?" He squinted at the spear and started polishing.

"It does," Brook said. *Maybe,* she thought, *just maybe, the magic has been waiting for someone to make things right.* And if she let herself go that far, well…maybe that someone was her.

The blue-faces were like a posse that grabbed all the best things for itself—chocolate milk or donated clothes or a whole box of sparkle pens—as soon as they saw you wanted them. A vicious clique that worked to make your life miserable and worse.

She'd do anything to stop them.

Fox cleared his throat.

Brook raised her eyebrows.

"The key gives us a chance," Fox said. "I don't know what we'll find inside, but if we catch the blues off guard, we can climb the tower and grab that key, and then…" He spread his hands, eyes big.

"Anything is possible." Something in Brook's chest fluttered.

"We could run this place," Fox said. "We could rule the castle."

"Like a king and queen," Brook said.

And they might have laughed, except they were both dead serious.

ONE LAST BATH BEFORE THE WAR

"WHAT WOULD YOU SAY TO SOME WEAPONS PRACTICE?" FOX SAID.

Brook thought it was a strange question for someone who didn't need to practice at all.

"Well, ok," she said.

"Just decide which of those weapons you favor, and let's spar," Fox said. "Mostly it's common sense."

Yeah right, Brook thought. Killing people like you're in a video game is not common sense. But I guess it's useful.

"I'll give you a few tips if I can," Fox said.

"*If* you can," she said. "Ha, thanks, Fox. You're so modest."

He gave a little bow. "By the way, how was that fight for you?"

"Uhh…" Brook said.

He wonders how you survived, she thought. Well!

"Guess I just got lucky," she said. "She tripped and I took a swing."

"Really?"

"Half of fighting *is* luck, don't you think?" she said to test her theory.

Fox didn't disagree, just raised one eyebrow. It could've meant anything.

Fine, Brook thought. I'll play it cool too if that's the way you're gonna be. You're not the only one who's good at games.

She picked up the scythe-staff. The handle tingled against her skin. Fox was touching everything in their weapons bank—a little theatrically, she thought.

"So many options!" Finally, he picked the axe. "Ok," he said. "Get ready."

Brook held the staff at waist height, hands loose, blade angled down to show she wasn't a threat. It made her think of a time, a moment, a memory—her holding her old Foundation shork loose in her fingertips, curled behind her wrist as she backed toward a wall—so no one would notice she was holding anything at all.

"You don't look very ready," Fox said.

"That's because you don't know how quick I–"

Wang!

"Ouch!" Brook yelped as the axehead connected with the top of her staff and sent vibrations through her hands. She snatched empty air as her weapon hit the moss.

"Gosh, my grip needs work, right?" She shook her fingers and laughed, trying to look just the right amount of embarrassed.

"See?" Fox said smugly.

"*You'll* see," Brook said. "When I kick your butt."

"Can't wait," Fox said.

She picked Isabella back up—now there's something she'd never reveal to Fox, that her weapon had a name—and tightened her grip. "Go ahead, try it again."

Fox swung the axe and this time she swooped her staff aside. He recovered and chopped again. She dodged a second time and smiled proudly.

"Good," Fox said, "Except–"

"Except what?" Brook frowned.

Fox threw down a flurry of two-handed chops. Brook jerked her staff right and left and managed to keep clear, but then she stumbled sideways and sat down hard.

"It's hard to fight from your rear," Fox said.

"Try not to be such a snot," Brook said.

They went a few more rounds, but things stayed about the same.

Fox grinned. He was really enjoying this.

Look at him, Brook thought. So happy I proved him right, like a cocky little kid.

It almost made her smile.

"Well, you're not so good at weapons," Fox said. "But how could you be? Did you know, I was worried you might assassinate me at one point? Haw!"

"Stop gloating," Brook said from the ground. "Just because you're all quick and—and foxy—doesn't mean everyone else is."

"My bad." He leaned the axe on one shoulder and stuck out a hand to help her up. She gave him a look—*this isn't even fair*—as he pulled her to her feet.

"All about repetition," he said. "Training your reflexes, keeping your balance, and getting stronger wrists."

"Wow, that sounds like a lot of work—wait." Brook put her hands behind her back. "What are you saying about my wrists?"

"Nothing, they're great," Fox said. "But you're not much of a threat yet, are you?" He smiled.

"Whatever," Brook said. "Maybe I was holding back."

"I'm sure you were."

"So"—Brook shook her head—"do you have any tips for me, or are you going to stand there grinning until your head explodes for the hundredth time?"

"Of course I have tips," Fox said. "I'm happy to share."

Brook rolled her eyes and maybe Fox would have given her some good advice—about how to grip the staff or how to keep her balance—if she hadn't scooped water from the pool, moving a lot faster than she had been, and splashed him in the face.

Fox gaped at her. Water dripped off his nose. Brook pressed a hand to her mouth, but it did no good. She laughed and laughed. And after that, sputtering and stamping around, Fox seemed to forget about the fighting tips. When Brook looked at him and raised her eyebrows, he shook his index finger at her.

"Uh uh, no more lessons for you today."

She tossed her head and felt a little disappointed. But it was definitely worth it.

They ate more jerky. After that, the day slowed down to nothing as they waited for the sun to set.

Fox seemed absent-minded. Mostly he jabbed at the ruined fire, not bothering to relight it. His eyes kept veering off into space and she knew what he was struggling with.

The castle. How they'd get in. What would happen.

She wanted to interrupt. She wanted to splash more water in his face so she could laugh at his expression—but she didn't. What did she know? The castle was gorgeous and the blue-faces were killers, *and maybe possibly there was hidden magic that would give them a hand.* What did Fox know? A whole lot more than that. So she left him alone with his plans, but the silence made for an endless afternoon.

Brook picked up each of the weapons in turn, hoping Fox would take the bait. He only glanced at her. She realized she wasn't sure where Dragon-Claw was, or Shark-Tooth, whatever she was calling it, which would've been unthinkable just yesterday. She'd obsessed over the little knife for days. After she'd wandered back and forth awhile, she found it in a pile of leaves near a boulder.

"There you are, Snake-Tooth," she said, and bent to grab it.

Fox didn't even look up.

For crying out loud, she was talking to a knife. Brook sighed. The afternoon was hot, even in the shade, and her skin felt flushed and sticky. She was tired of thinking about the castle. She'd be dreaming about it all night. Monique and her mean girls would shove her out of her bunk, and she'd lash out with her shork and fly into the castle, where she'd run downstairs into a scary, low-lit basement, lined with washers and dryers where the dragon would be waiting.

Brook stopped playing with Viper-Fang. "I'm going to the creek. I need a bath."

"Mmhm," Fox said. "Oh, you're leaving? Be careful, Brook. Keep your eyes open. I can't afford to lose you. Actually, I could use a wash too. I'll come along. Don't worry, separate corners of the creek. You can have the one from last time."

"Fine," Brook said.

Whatever Fox was planning, it had better be good. She was getting tired of his schemy spaciness. They walked past the rock formation and around the swamp, then dove into the thicket without discussing the dragon-scorched hillside. When they shoved their way onto the open, Fox headed north.

"Yell if you need me," he said. "I'll be close enough to hear."

Brook sniffed.

He held his hands up as he walked away.

She scrambled through the leafy curtain and down the bank to the pebbled shore. Getting clean would be easier now that she had her system figured out. She slipped out of her clothes, waded into the stream and scrubbed them. She hung them up to dry and splashed back in to scrub herself. Then she started to shiver, but not because she was cold. The water was refreshing.

This could be my last bath, she thought. Tomorrow I could be dead.

Fox was good, very good, but they had no idea what they were getting into. All those blue-faces. Waiting in the castle like Pit Bulls. Did it really make sense? Maybe we could find another campsite, she thought. What if we kept on living the way we are?—except the way we're living is awful.

It wasn't like they'd been careless. Fox was the opposite of careless. And look at how close to death they'd come. Running and hiding, tracked and ambushed.

Kinda like her years at the Foundation.

Maybe this is hell, she thought. Maybe I'm being punished in a kind of endless loop.

Maybe I deserve to be here.

But no, hell wouldn't have a place like the castle. And she and Fox were starting to be friends. She couldn't remember the last time she'd laughed without using the laughter to hide something else. You didn't laugh like that in hell. Not to mention, there wouldn't be even a hint of magic. Magic that opened a door and sent you to a bad place, but for a good reason, so that something happy had a chance of happening.

Please let there be magic, she thought.

"Please God, let there be magic," she whispered, and then because it seemed like the right thing: "Please God, send me magic, even though I don't deserve it."

She sat in the brook with water gurgling around her and wondered if God was listening.

It's worth fighting for, she thought. You have a chance at things you've never had your whole life, at least since your parents stopped loving you. It's worth the risk. And living on this island, surviving a day at a time, those aren't great odds anyway.

What's another day playing chicken with death?

Why not, if maybe something good could happen?

But it was hard to think of her life as something that could be used up. Poured out, a drop at a time. Emptied. And now the thought had crossed her mind, it kept creeping back in:

What if you deserve to be here, and not for a good reason?

What if you're being punished?

The water felt colder on her skin.

This brook leaks underground, she thought. It drips through

rocks and caves and it touches the ocean—it must. So the sea, right now, is touching me. Trickling hungrily over my bones while I'm trying to get clean.

She knew the island was smiling again, teeth gleaming in the current, eyes watching from the darkness under rocks. Grinning at her.

It had never stopped.

WHAT YOU DON'T KNOW CAN HURT YOU

BROOK PULLED HER DAMP CLOTHES BACK ON AND STARTED BACK without looking for Fox.

Maybe there were more hit-kids out there, but it seemed unlikely they were searching the forest. She and Fox—well, mostly Fox—had crushed them. The rest of the blue-faces had to know something had gone badly wrong with their plan.

"Now they're nervous," Brook told the trees as she marched up the slope. She liked the way she sounded. Confident and deadly, a girl who could change a whole battle just by showing up. It wasn't at all the way she felt.

"I'm *soo* dangerous," she said in the same cool, breezy voice. "They'll never see it coming. Fox will get us inside, total stealth mode, and then, *Brook unleashed*. We'll take the key. If they get in our way, they'll wish they hadn't."

She stopped on the edge of the dragon scorch area, searching the sky. Five minutes went by, and when nothing moved except clouds, she gulped down a breath and shot into the open. Crunching through the ashes, she flew over blackened logs, dodging right and left until she reached the safe green shadows.

"Still got it," she gasped, brushing back her hair with her fingertips.

Brook found her way back to the campsite on autopilot. Inside their hollow she took a drink and stood there, admiring their weapons bank. Black and silver gleamed against the rocks. A row of spiky, razor-sharp death.

On this island it was worth a fortune.

Since Fox still wasn't back, she picked up the scythe-staff and did a few made-up drills, quick and quiet, focusing on her footwork. She stopped when she felt the first drop of sweat run down her back, because who knew when she'd get another bath?

She cut that thought off short.

By then she was hungry. At least her stomach was sending her signals, and she'd probably need the strength. She found the jerky easily, piled in a shady crack. Only a few dried strips of meat were left.

"Here's hoping our lives change fast," Brook said.

For a split second, she thought about heading to the rabbit runs or the coast to look for food. Then she pictured a gang of killer kids waiting on the edge of the forest, picking their teeth with their knives.

Being hungry would keep her alert.

Brook tore off a small piece of jerky and chewed slowly, pretending it was gum. She traced the grain of the stone wall with her eyes. The storage crack was a deep one. If they were staying, they could've stored their new weapons with the jerky. All those blades in the open were asking for trouble. She picked up Isabella and trailed the blade of her scythe-staff down the crack. It would easily fit inside.

The dark zig-zag in the rock face became a shallow cave. There was a lot of shade inside. Maybe raccoons or possums had lived there. If it had rained again like it had her first night, it would've been a good idea to crawl inside. She wondered if Fox knew the crack became a gap.

Clink went the blade of her staff.

She stopped with her head at an angle. Shading her eyes with one hand, she picked out a vague, pale gleam.

"Oh great," she said. "More bones."

When she'd found the skull under the fire, she'd guessed the rest of the skeleton was down there too. So what was this? Had Fox run out of room? How many feral kids had he burnt and buried?

She bit her lip and reached inside. If she came up with a rib or leg bone, she wouldn't scream. Fox wasn't stupid. The bones would be clean and sterilized. Her fingers closed on something cool to the touch and not as grainy as she'd expected. Cartilage? But cartilage would melt, wouldn't it?

What a gross question.

"No big deal," she said.

She pulled the slim bone into the light.

But it wasn't a bone.

The dagger had two blades, one on either side of a pale handle, and it was a good thing she'd grabbed the handle. The blades gleamed bluish-gray, like they'd been oiled moments before. She knew they'd slice her skin like she was made of paper.

A minute before, she'd been worried about sweating after her bath. Now ice-cold worms squirmed up and down her spine, wriggling like night crawlers after rain. Her fingers trembled. How could Fox have done this? And there was more. Leaning forward over the stone edge, she pulled weapon after weapon from the trove.

A brutal spiked hammer.

A pair of straight, two-edged knives.

A curvy sword.

A spear with a spiked blade on one side.

A bow and a bunch of arrows in a leather bag.

A whole zoo of gleaming, bladed death.

Fox, how could you? Her knees felt weak. He could've given her a weapon anytime, and instead he'd pretended they only had a sword—and a little knife. What was wrong with him? What had he been planning with all these weapons? Where had he found them and who had he taken them from?

She shuddered. Jumbled on the moss, they glittered in a lethal pile. She wondered if she should put them back. Could she hold it together when Fox walked in? Could she pretend this hadn't happened, that he wasn't a liar? That he wasn't... well, *what* was he? What had he done?

"I can do it," Brook said. "I can hold it together."

It will be better that way, she thought. You need to buy some time, decide what to do next, tease out what Fox is up to.

She picked up the spear on the top of the pile and slid it back into the cave.

A shadow fell across her back.

MASTER OF EVERY SITUATION

Brook turned slowly.

Fox looked pale.

They stared at each other for a long moment. She took in his gray eyes, his damp, reddish hair. The mouth that could change so fast into a smile. The freckles on his nose. He always looked so confident, the master of every situation. Now he looked like someone had taken all his words away.

Fox sat down in a bed of moss, one of the few clean patches, and put his face in his hands. Brook slid one foot under a mace. She gave it a soccer lift and and caught it, squeezing the handle tight.

"Who are you?" She hadn't meant to whisper. She'd meant to sound strong and cool like she had in the woods. Instead, she clenched the mace even harder, until her knuckles turned white.

"I'm sorry, Brook," Fox croaked. "I'm sorry."

She stood there, wondering if he had a dagger in his lap. All he'd have to do was glance up, measure the distance, flick his wrist. She'd seen what he could do.

Still looking at the ground, he spread his hands. "You have a right to be angry."

Brook's face tingled like all the blood had drained away.

"Yeah," she said.

"I—I'm compulsive," Fox said. "I've been that way forever. I want all the weapons. I want all the angles. It makes me feel like I'm in charge."

"Not good enough," Brook said, since they were being honest. "You said you liked me. You said you wanted me on your team. Now I see that if I hadn't taken the scythe-staff, I'd probably still be begging you to let me carry the knife. 'Can I borrow it, Foxy?'"

She winced. "And if I'd known about all this, if I'd found it when I got here, I wonder what you would've said? 'Sorry, Brook, we need to keep you safe. I don't want you to cut yourself. Let's just keep all the swords and the spears and the hammer and the axe and the bow and the thing with two blades—"

"The haladie," Fox said.

"Right, let's hide all this stuff away in my weapons stash. And then, Brook, if you're very, very good—maybe I'll let you use a sword to poke the fire."

Fox finally looked up. His wet eyes flamed to life.

"Yeah," he said. "Ok. There's something not right with me, that holds on to every little thing. Even though I like you, it almost killed me to give you the knife, I admit it. My brain was screaming, *No no no!* when I handed it over. I'm even jealous of your scythe-staff because—" He blinked and took a breath.

"I've never been wanted, Brook. Never been wanted. I'm pretty sure I already told you but I lose track. I'm not supposed to be here, and I don't mean the island. I mean alive. I'm not supposed to be drawing breaths or taking up space. I don't remember anything about my past, but I know this one thing. It's in my bones. My parents tried to kill me."

He touched the spear he'd set down in the moss.

"Tried to kill me before they saw me. Crazy, huh? They

hated me automatically. Can you believe that? There's a word for it, and you could probably tell me, but a few minutes later, I'd forget." He tapped his head. "Somehow, my parents didn't get to murder me. They must have been so disappointed! But I know they tried and I'll always know. I'll never, ever forget."

Fox was breathing hard. He looked like he'd run a race. Brook knew the word he was looking for but she didn't say it. She didn't say anything. What was there to say?

"I'm sorry," Fox said again. "I wish I was different. I wish I wasn't so on edge. I wish I didn't always expect to be attacked."

"This isn't right," Brook said. "What your parents tried to do to you—and this. This is horrible, just horrible. Someone like you should never be in a place like this."

Fox looked in her face. "No one should be in a place like this," he said. "You shouldn't be here either, Brook. You were abandoned too."

His voice became less shaky. He rubbed a wrist across his eyes, and when he took his hand away, they had dried back up.

"You're right, neither of us deserve this," Brook said. "Whoever did this will pay."

She'd been so angry with Fox and now she just felt sick. She set the mace down on top of the pile. All the weapons gleamed and shone. Spikes and blades and edges of all kinds. A shiny carnival of death. She felt like they were pointing at her and Fox. Maybe they'd been pointed at them their entire lives.

"We'll get the castle," Brook said. "Then we'll decide what to do. Maybe we need to go after the dragon."

Fox nodded. "Right. I don't think anyone's tried that yet."

They split the last of the jerky, barely a mouthful each.

"Maybe I'll go check the snares," Fox said.

"Do you think that's a good idea?"

"No." He smiled. "But we have a few hours and we need to eat. By tomorrow, we'll be inside the castle and everything will be different."

"I'll come with you," Brook said.

"Let me go. I'll be faster alone."

She didn't agree. A cool breeze skimmed the back of her neck, saying something bad would happen if they separated. But she nodded. She felt heavy and still inside, like she could lean back against the standing stones and maybe the granite would soak into her and she'd become part rock.

She wished she had the right words for Fox, words that would make things better, but those words didn't exist. Fox wanted to pull himself together. She'd never seen him cry before, and she couldn't imagine what he was feeling. He sure hid a lot behind that smile.

"I'll make a fire," she said.

"Sounds good." He grabbed a weapon from the pile, barely looking at it, and disappeared.

Brook leaned her head against the stone and coolness flowed through her cropped hair. The weight of the whole dark island pressed on her. How could a place like this exist? The worst possible place for people like her and Fox. The worst kind of place for anyone.

What do the blue-faces know? she wondered. What have they figured out? Maybe there are secrets in the castle. Maybe the blues have promises from the dragon. Who knows what we'll discover when we get inside?

But as hard as she tried to keep her mind busy, she couldn't stop thinking about Fox's words: Never wanted, Brook, never wanted.

Probably the worst words you could ever hear. And they weren't just true about Fox.

They are true about me.

It left her feeling weak, leaning on the rock until the emptiness in her chest flared up like dragon fire. Her parents, whoever they were, had made a mistake. The great mistake of their lives. If they ever met her, it would be too late. By then she'd have proved she was someone who mattered, someone tough and charming, a girl who impressed everyone, who everyone liked and wished they knew.

She and Fox would start with the castle.

They'd prove everyone wrong.

The blue-faces wouldn't know what hit them.

She wiped her eyes and gathered up some kindling.

By the time Fox got back with a rabbit, she'd kindled her own fire in the middle of their ruined campsite. Might as well be comfortable their final night.

PLAN OF ATTACK

"Here's how it will go," Fox said.

He seemed to have recovered his confidence after his trip to the fields, and there wasn't a trace of choky wetness in his voice. Brook chewed her rabbit and listened. She thought about how angry she was and how things were going to go well.

"We'll cross the plains by moonlight," Fox said. "With a little luck, they won't see us coming. We'll reach the castle while it's still dark and find the door. Not the front door, the back one. Then I'll get somewhere out of sight and you'll knock."

"Why would they open for me?" Brook said.

"You'll pretend to be hurt so they won't think you're a threat."

"And?" She shrugged.

"And—you'll have a weapon with you. More than one."

"Ohhh." Brook almost smiled. "I'll carry some of your treasure as bait."

"Yeah." Fox didn't realize she was joking. "But it'll be worth it. Anyway, we'll get it back."

"So they see poor, sad, injured me, and more importantly, the weapons I'm carrying, and they open up?"

"That's right," Fox said. "Probably just one of them. It'll be early, so I don't expect too many will be up. Let's say one blue is on guard, and he sees you, a weak girl, acting all hurt, and he sees the weapons and his eyes light up. He's not going to call for help. He'll want them for himself."

"Uh huh," Brook said. "Me, a weak girl, thanks for clarifying that."

"That's what *he* thinks," Fox said. "But instead, we grab him."

"And we lock him outside." Brook pictured them slamming the door on the horrified blue-face, then turning to race up stone steps into the castle, higher and higher, into pale moonlight with just a trace of yellow in the eastern sky. "What if there's more than one guard?" she said.

"Even if there is, we'll have a chance," Fox said.

Brook thought about the bodies in the woods and knew he was right. *We'll always have a chance.*

"Then we're in, and it's still mostly dark, and maybe we'll find some face paint, but even if we don't, we start searching for the key."

"In the top of the highest tower," Brook said.

"Right."

"It's a plan I guess." She hugged herself and thought, What did you expect?

After they ate, Fox leaned all the weapons in a row against the rock face. The collection was scary and impressive. He lined them up on Brook's side, which was obviously an apology and possibly flattery, and she appreciated it, even though she couldn't bring herself to thank him.

With so many options in front of her, all she really needed was Isabella and maybe the little knife—Snake-Tooth or Viper-Fang, whatever she was calling it. She didn't need a whole arsenal like Fox seemed to think he did.

She sat by the fire, which probably had chalky bones under it, and stayed warm as the sun went down. Night birds began to shriek. Something howled far away and was joined by another howl, and another.

Death Dogs, talking to each other in the night.

"Do you think this will work?" she asked Fox.

The wall between them had mostly come down again.

He sat across the fire, feeding it small twigs and shoving it around with the sword. "Yes," he said. "It has to work and the two of us—we're unstoppable." He gave her a smile.

"Yeah. Unstoppable is us."

A few minutes later, she did her best to fall asleep. Thin lines of sunset dripped through crisscrossed trees, neon orange sinking in a pool of liquid cotton candy. The sunset was probably an eight point five, but she bumped it to a ten to show the island she wasn't scared. She told herself *this* sunset would always be one of her favorites.

Brook woke when it was still dark. Maybe Fox had touched her. Maybe it was just his movement nearby. She was instantly alert. Moonlight filtered through the trees like milky flashlight beams. She got up and stretched. Her mind was already racing.

Had they overslept? Did they have enough time to reach the castle?

"Ready when you are," Fox said in a hushed voice, like miles away the blue-faces might hear them. Water dripped off his chin, and Brook stepped over to take her turn at the pool. She rinsed her mouth and face and took a drink, then joined Fox by their shining row of weapons. The sharp edges gleamed under the moon.

Fox's face looked pinched, and she realized what was bothering him. There was no way they could carry everything. They'd have to leave some weapons behind. For him it was like leaving a pile of cash blowing in the wind.

Brook took Isabella and Dragon-Tooth from the moss. She'd kept them close while she slept. "Maybe we can come back for the rest," she said.

"Yeah," Fox said. "After we win."

He chose a battle-axe and a spear. "Better take something else for yourself," he said. "To make sure the blue-faces open the door."

"Oh," Brook said. "Right." She picked up a sword, realized how hard it would be to carry, and set it down. Instead she chose the trident. Less likely to slice her by mistake.

"I'm ready," she said. "Go team."

And just like that they set off, leaving the smoky wisps of their fire in the air. Brook didn't let herself look back. This is it, she thought. The chance to get everything you want. Quiet, safety, space. A high window. A locked door. You and Fox will take over, and everyone will see what you can do. Please God, let there be magic.

They stole through the woods like ghosts. Brook felt the cool night breeze on the back of her neck. She kept her eyes wide open as they crept under trees through pools of shadow. Before she knew it, they'd reached the plains. The sky lightened but there was no trace of the sun. A full moon hung like a big opal over the fields. In the distance, something howled.

Brook froze at the edge of the forest.

"It's ok," Fox said. "They're miles away. And it sounds like they're already on the hunt."

She nodded and followed him into the open. Fox began to jog, his spear and axe pressed to his shoulders. He wove toward the rabbit run.

"Hey!" Brook whispered loudly. "Where are you going?"

Fox's shadow swerved in the glimmering dark. She realized he was running backward, high-stepping like he was in track and field.

"Rabbits," he called in a low voice. "One last time."

That didn't make sense to Brook, but she didn't have Fox's compulsions. She picked up her pace, Isabella and the trident held against her shoulder blades, Snake-Tooth at her hip. Fox knew the fields by heart and by the time she caught him, he'd dodged down the worn run and bent over a snare. The blades of his weapons gleamed.

"Fox," she hissed, "what are you doing?"

He pulled a dead rabbit from the trap and glanced at her. It was hard to read his face in the shadow of the moon. "Sorry," he said. "But we need a little blood to make this whole thing work. You need to look hurt, remember?"

"Ohh..." Brook said.

Of course. She was impressed by how carefully he'd planned this, and ticked off at herself for not thinking ahead. *Wake up, Brook. Stay on top of things.*

Fox pulled a knife from his pocket and slit the rabbit open.

"Do you really want to do that here?" She scanned the gently waving grass. Thanks to the moon, it was like standing in a sea of silver. The breeze smelled like the ocean and it wasn't a comforting smell. The salty tang made her think of hungry cliffs. Of the island watching. Of time ticking away.

"Better here than by the castle," Fox said through gritted teeth.

Blood drip-dripped in a dark puddle at his feet.

"I don't have free hands to carry it," he said. "So I'll have to tuck its paws into my pocket. Crap, this isn't easy."

Brook was turning in place by now. Grass rustled. A bird screamed in the night. Something squeaked in the grass.

"Fox, let's–" Then she heard the sound she was dreading. The one she didn't want to hear, the one that could ruin their plan, that could ruin everything.

A Death Dog howled. It was closer, she was sure.

"Give me that rabbit." Brook snatched it from him and the blood ran warm on her hands. She bit her lip and touched her face. No, not enough. She pulled her fingers down her cheeks, keeping it away from her eyes. She could smell the blood as well as feel it, slick and hot and coppery, coating her skin. She shook her fingers, flicking the stickiness away, happy she couldn't see herself.

"Ok, can we go now?"

Fox looked at her and nodded. "That should do it." He dropped the rabbit and moved away, shoes squishing in the grass. A Death Dog howled somewhere to the south, joined by another and another. Fox looked concerned.

"Now we'd better run," he said.

CATCH ME IF YOU CAN

IN WEED, BROOK HAD WANTED TO RUN TRACK. NO ONE HAD EVER told her she was fast but she had a feeling, based on experience. Sports passes were really hard to come by, though. No one at the Foundation wanted to deal with the headache of a kid who stayed after school and whose movements would have to be documented when she practiced and traveled who knew where for track meets.

If only she'd been allowed to run track, maybe she could've run faster toward the castle, over the ghostly plains with the Death Dogs on her trail.

They'd barely even left their camp and nothing was going right. Nothing. The hard metal of Isabella and the trident jolted Brook's shoulders, sliding back and forth as she tried to keep them upright. Her face was hot and sticky, slick with sweat and blood. At the same time, the wind chilled her arms and legs, mocking her with memories of the cliffs.

You thought you got away, the island was saying. *Thought you could save your guts and bones from me. But it was just a small delay. I'll win, one way or another...*

Fox was pulling away and that was the last thing Brook

wanted. Heart slamming her ribs, she made her feet move faster. Their journey had started as a jog and climbed quickly to a run. If they went any faster, it would be a sprint. When clouds floated over the moon, all she could do was keep moving in the same direction.

It's inevitable, the island whispered. *Whether it's the breakers or the rocks or the Death Dogs, you'll be mine...*

Her feet pounded over dead stalks and animal mounds. No matter how hard she tried, she couldn't catch her breath. Gasping, gasping. Would she ever breathe again?

The wind swirled and danced, grabbing the air right out of her mouth.

You can't outrun me, the island said. *I've had you since you crawled onto the sand. No one ever really gets away.*

She pictured the island smiling.

Its teeth were jagged coral. Its eyes were sunken caves.

Its belly was the bottom of the sea.

Maybe this is where it ends, Brook thought between gasps. You did your best—the best you possibly could—but now it's all caught up with you. Your knees will give out and you'll fall— maybe you'll hit your head—and the Death Dogs will get here— and you'll be dead.

Like those other kids, dead.

Then, somehow, they rounded the corner of the forest. The north side of the island opened in front of them, wide and pale, and the castle loomed into the sky. Huge. Impossibly big and black. Brook couldn't believe how close they were.

Her lungs decided not to collapse. Her legs agreed to keep working. She skimmed through the grass, flashing down rabbit runs, flying toward the castle's shadow. It got taller and taller, high notched walls and soaring towers. Brook wasn't aware of breathing anymore. Her lungs had stopped needing air. Now there was just the *thwack, thwack, thwack* of her feet over the fields and the weapons thunking against her bones, same as the pounding of her heart.

She blinked salt out of her eyes. Fox was just ahead.

Then the deep shade of the castle fell on her like a blanket. They'd done it. They'd made it. Now everything would be ok. Brook realized her lungs were shriveling up, screaming for oxygen. She dropped the trident and put a hand to her side as pain knifed her ribs. "Ohhh—oww."

"C'mon, Brook." Fox was wheezing too. "Don't stop, we've gotta get inside." Juggling his own weapons, he groaned and bent to grab her trident.

Brook forced herself to take it. But when she touched the metal, her fingers were warm and wet. Oh no. When she looked down, the corner of her hip pocket was dark. Snake-Tooth had cut her. Snake-Tooth had *turned* on her. The little knife was supposed to be on her side. It was almost more than she could handle.

"Brook!" Fox's hands were on her shoulders. His smoky eyes burned into hers.

She knew he was doing everything he could to bring her along. Listen to him, she thought. Trust him completely, just this once.

"I'm coming," she said. "Show me."

An eerie howl drifted over the plains, broken by hungry, sharp-edged barks.

"They're close," Fox said. "But we're closer."

A massive front gate rose on their left, tall as trees, studded with metal bands and spikes. The moon gleamed on the timbers. On the right, the blue-black wall of the castle curved away.

Fox squeezed her cold hand. "Follow me."

The darkness was so thick, Brook felt like they were pushing through it. When she looked up, trying to slow her breathing, she saw black rectangles high on the giant walls. But down on the ground, in the high grass, night folded down on them. The dark side of the castle felt like the dark side of the moon.

Brook folded an arm across her chest and clasped her weapons awkwardly so she could slide a hand into her pocket. She prayed that Snake-Tooth hadn't bit too deep. She found the dagger's handle and pulled. A corner of its carrying cloth was torn and soaked with blood. But just a corner. The pain in her hip felt like a pin-prick and she hoped that's what it was, but she didn't have time to check.

Fox stopped under a jutting stone slab. At some point they'd turned a corner, because the moon was shining bright again. Stone steps rose from the grass, and Brook realized she was looking at a sheltered porch. Back in California, it was the kind of place homeless people would be sleeping. A metal-plated door stood at the top. In the center of the door was a thin slit.

"This is it," Fox whispered. "It's your time, Brook. Knock and tell them you're hurt. Don't think too hard, just do it."

Her heart was beating so loud, she wondered if she'd even need to knock. But she could hear the wind again, howling in the castle's towers. Except—no, that wasn't the wind. The howls were jagged and eager. Brook stumbled up the stairs and pounded on the door.

Doom, doom, doom. It echoed in the night like a rusty gong.

She took a breath and pounded again.

Doom, doom, doom.

"Keep knocking," Fox whispered from the shadows. She couldn't see him, but she pictured him clutching his spear and axe, staring at the door.

Brook raised her hand to knock again and almost screamed. A pair of wide eyes appeared in the narrow window. They got even bigger when they took in her bloody face.

"Are you hurt bad?" The boy's voice sounded squeaky from sleep.

Brook held up her weapons and leaned them against the

wall, making sure the boy could see. She opened her mouth to say, Yes, yes, I'm hurt so bad I might not ever get better, but instead, a sob rose from her throat. She scrubbed at her face and her knuckles came away red and wet.

"Oh no." The kid's eyes looked horrified. "I'm not supposed to open this, ever."

Brook forced herself to look up as tears rolled down her face. She didn't understand what was happening. He wasn't reacting the way a blue-face should, even though she could see dark swirls of paint around his eyes. He wasn't staring greedily at her weapons. What was he doing? Why wasn't he taking the bait?

"Please help me," Brook said. "I can't run anymore."

His eyes flicked right and left. Surely he knew the weapons were worth a fortune—he had to, had to. The boy groaned and the thin strip of his face disappeared. Brook sagged against the wall in defeat. Now you've got to be deadly and smart, she told herself. Now you've got to fight the monsters.

Metal rasped on the far side of the door. Bolts sliding open, lots of them. Old hinges screamed in protest as the door scraped open

inch

after inch

after inch

until the boy looked through an opening barely wider that his head.

He held out one hand.

"Quick," he said. "What if he's out there, waiting for–"

Then everything happened.

WHAT HAPPENED AT THE DOOR

THE BLUE-FACED BOY SCREAMED.

It made no sense. Brook hadn't tried to scare him. She hadn't lunged at him or made a grab for the door, even though she desperately wanted to get inside. Then she saw blood gushing from his upper leg—splashing on the stone at his feet. For a second, she couldn't make sense of it. She hadn't done this. This wasn't the Foundation basement, where there'd been a lot of blood—so much blood. Then the boy kicked Fox's spear away, and it fell clunking down the stairs.

"Fox, quick–" she started to say, but the blue-face was closing the door.

"No!" Brook threw herself forward, stuck her arm and shoulder through, and shrugged the door wider. Just like that, she was in.

Inside the castle. She couldn't believe it.

Thank God, she thought. Everything is about to change.

The boy backed away. His shoulders slumped, and when he held up his hands, they trembled. "Please, let me go." He turned and stumbled off, favoring his bloody leg.

This blue-face isn't fierce at all, Brook thought. *All the time he's spent getting everything his way has made him soft. Pitiful, and it will make things a lot easier.* She wasn't even holding Isabella.

"In," Brook breathed. "We're in, in, in!"

"Brook, hang on a second," Fox shouted.

She stuck her head through the door to grab her scythe-staff and laughed. "Are you crazy? Get in here!"

Fox could've been a silver statue in the moonlight. Then he moved toward her, sliding his weapons to one shoulder. "Hang on a second." He climbed the stairs. With his free hand, he reached for her through the doorway.

"No!" Brook stepped away. "Are you crazy?" She felt a flash of anger, more than a flash, because she'd almost died getting here. Death Dogs were closing in, and the door was open— against all odds, open!—and Fox was loitering in the dark.

"I'm going on," she said. "Something good just happened, something crazy good. Are you awake? Can you believe this? I'm going after the key, so stop trying to grab me."

She turned and shot away after the bleeding boy, holding Isabella at an angle to the stairs.

"Brook, wait!" Fox yelled.

She pretended not to hear him. Was he seriously gonna freeze up now? *Now,* when they had the edge, and he'd never been scared before? Well, she'd do it all then. It was her plan too, as much as his and maybe more. Getting in had been her idea first. She was the one who knew about the magic, who was ready to be a hero. She'd go alone.

She'd find the key herself.

The stones under her feet were wide and smooth. She flew up a long, straight flight of stairs like they were nothing. At the top, she stood on a wide landing where stars gleamed through a window. More stairs led off in three directions—and the place felt perfect, she thought, so huge and safe and strong.

She leaned on the windowsill, which—oh gross—was coated with cobwebs, a thick layer of grime and tiny bones. All the luxury had made the blue-faces lazy. *She* wouldn't be lazy. Dirt could be scrubbed. Cobwebs swept away. Not a big job, just a bucket of water and a rag, a whole lot more rewarding than cleaning the cracked Foundation floors.

And now, onward!

Night wind brushed her face and swept her hair. She tossed her head, pushed a few strands behind one ear, and whispered, "This is who I am now. An adventurer. An explorer of castles. No, not castles—*my* castle."

She took another flight of stairs, up, up, up, searching for the highest tower. No one tried to stop her—the rest of the blue-faces were taking their time, which was perfect. She felt like she was racing over a rooftop while their heads were turned, her timing and her moves just right. She was about to get away with something *huge*. But as she went, she noticed a trail of drips and smears which she didn't like. It meant the injured blue-face was close by.

That made her think, Where's Fox? He should have caught up by now. But at the same time, she felt happy he wasn't there. Because now this was her heist. *Her* chance. Excitement hummed and darted in her chest like the tiny, shining birds that lived on nectar.

She was pulling off this crazy scheme alone.

It would make the castle *hers*. And let's be honest, she thought. This makes you really cool. If you pull it off, Fox will be so impressed. He'll know what you can do, no more wondering. No more secrets. You'll have proved your worth on Team Brook-Fox, helping him for once. After this, he'll like you even more. So do as much as you possibly can.

Get past the blue-faces.

Find the key.

Be the queen.

By the time Fox caught up, she'd be on a big throne, eating chicken and splashing her feet in clear, cold water. The blue-faces would be lined up, asking if there was anything else she needed. Queen of the castle. *Hey Fox, you finally got here,* she'd say. *Good thing I saved you a seat.*

That made her smile.

Then, without meaning to, she found the boy.

He crouched on the floor in the corner of another landing. A wooden torch flickered on the wall. The boy was struggling with his shirt, tugging it over his head, and he didn't look good. When he saw Brook, he froze in a huddled pile.

More good luck, she thought. *He's not a threat at all.*

"Why'd you do it?" he croaked. "Why'd you open the door for him?"

"You shouldn't have shut us out!" Brook shot back. *Here I am, ghosting up the stairs, conquering your castle like it's nothing, with magic opening doors for me. Why resist us?*

The boy was trying to wind the shirt around his bloody leg. He was having trouble knotting it. His fingers kept shaking.

"Not so tough now, huh?" she said. "Not when there's only one of you. Let me tie that, then you can show me the highest tower."

His eyes twitched toward her and away. "Why?"

"So I can get the key, of course," Brook said.

And look around and choose my room, she thought.

The boy shrugged. "Ok."

Wow, not even an argument. Handing her the castle, just like that. Brook hid a smile. She knelt beside him, wrapped the shirt around his leg and knotted it tight. The cut looked nasty and she stopped holding her breath once it was covered up.

"There you go," she said, and stood. "Sorry Fox did that, but you can't blame him, the way all of you have treated us."

The boy blinked. He started laughing, not a happy laugh.

And Brook noticed how skinny he was, skin and bones, really, and very dirty, covered in dust and stains. And he smelled bad too.

"Are you a servant for the real blue-faces or something?" she asked. "Do they make you do stuff they don't want to, like watch the door? Because—"

You don't look like the ruler of a castle, she wanted to say.

The kid looked up and finally met her eyes. "You're not kidding, are you?" The mask of blue paint was cracking and falling away in bits, and all at once it hit her: The paint wasn't supposed to cause fear. It was supposed to hide fear.

And it wasn't working.

Was she really that scary?

"Look," the boy said. "I don't know who you are, but you're really turned around. Go away. Run as fast as you can. Now that you've let him in, it's just a matter of time before he comes after all of us."

"What?" Brook stared down at him. "Who comes after us? You mean Fox?"

The boy smiled bitterly. "Around here we call him Wolf."

Brook took a sharp breath. So what if they do? she thought. Fox to his friends, Wolf to his enemies. A good kind of friend to have. She crossed her arms.

The boy didn't notice, pulling himself to his feet.

"Just point me to the highest tower," she said.

"You don't want to go there," the boy said.

"Where is it?" Brook snapped.

He pointed. "Up, always up. You'll get there sooner than you'd like." He paused. "I'm sorry for you."

Brook glared at him. *What a liar*, she thought. *Trying to trick me because he doesn't have the guts to fight. But some of his friends will, if I give them the chance.* Then she was flying up the stairs. Scuffling steps and a shout came from a side passage as she shot past. Another landing, another window. Outside, an open sea of black. And another landing and another—but something had changed.

Her grippy trail shoes scrabbled through trash. The shadows

hid most of it, but what she saw made her feel sick. Crusty rags. Broken weapons. Fragments of bone. When wind sailed through the windows, it no longer felt clean. If felt hungry, like the wind out on the cliffs.

Her stomach twisted.

Then, without warning, she reached the highest tower.

THE BASEMENT

BROOK SKIDDED TO A STOP, ARMS FLAILING, AND HALF-FELL backward. She stood on a dead-end balcony with no railings and a view to nowhere. The moon shone down through a huge stone silo, open to the sky. Empty walls rose another forty feet and plummeted down she couldn't say how far. No rooms, no stairs. No key hanging from a hook. Just hollow nothingness. Another step and she'd have fallen into the pitch-black pit—a man-made version of the cliffs. The castle's heart was an open elevator shaft.

A rotten hole. A giant trap.

No wonder the island was laughing.

Brook wanted to cry.

Standing there in the hushed emptiness, she felt her vision of the castle crumble and fall away. Roaches scuttled on the walls. Trash blew in the wind. She heard sounds above her, below her, behind the stone, and knew she was hearing rats. Hungry and hiding, living off scraps. The magnificent fortress in her mind was nothing but a ruin.

She thought she would suffocate.

Breathe, in and out, breathe.

She felt like she was back in Weed, under bare bulbs and a low, dirty ceiling. This time the memory from her dreams took over. She had nothing left to fight it with.

Pain shot up her spine, jarred the back of her skull as she hit the dormitory floor. Monique's gang stood over her, tossing her blanket and sheets—their way of showing they saw her trying to keep her head down—and it didn't work. They were cussing and searching for the shork that was somehow in her hand. She could've slid it in her waistband and lay there until her head stopped ringing. She could've closed her eyes and pretended to be somewhere else, *someone* else. Sometimes it worked, and when you woke up, the danger was gone.

But she was too angry and hurt to think.

When she lashed out with the shork, someone screamed and staggered back. Then Brook was up and running crookedly through the dorm, shoving off the double row of bunks with all the girls fake-sleeping. One hand on her head, she picked up speed as she ran down the low-lit hall. Curses and pounding feet came after her.

There was no one you could go to after dark, not with people hunting you, not in a hurry. She rushed down sticky corridors and creaky stairs, through the echoing rec room, shoving folding chairs out of the way—and then she made her great mistake.

She could've doubled back. She could've ducked into a closet. Instead, her head still ringing, she swerved into the darkness of the basement where she liked to hide, where she'd wedged herself between the washers and dryers to read *The Lord of the Flies.*

But no one had been chasing her then.

She'd barely hidden when Monique's gang crashed down the stairs. They found her in moments and closed in, cussing, one of them limping. Monique, big-boned and crazy, clenched a broken bottle.

"Hands over your head, Rapunzel," she hissed. "Always prepping, tidying, acting all better."

"No," Brook said. "No, I don't–"

"Did I say you could talk?" Monique sneered. "Let's make sure you don't act better anymore. Hands up."

No way, Brook thought. Not a chance—in the guts of the Foundation, on the stained concrete, under the bare lightbulbs. No one to hear me, no one to find me—no one to do a thing. She backed away.

"Ohh, you *do* think you're better."

A washing machine cut into Brook's back as the half circle closed in. Monique lunged, her eyes wild. Brook tried to dodge but there was no room. The bottleneck reached out like a jagged green mouth and bit her. She held back a scream. Panic pounded in her chest as hot blood trickled through her fingers. A red haze of pain spread under her hand when she pressed her hip.

Maybe now it's over, she thought. All I did was cut someone's leg.

Maybe now we're even.

"Gotcha." Monique's pupils glittered. "Not so lively now, are you?"

"Stop, I–"

Monique laughed and came at Brook again.

She never knew when to stop.

Palms pressed against the washer, Brook brought up her knees and drove her feet into Monique's stomach. The tall girl choked and doubled over. Brook pressed a hand to her burning side and tried to limp away. But no. The other girls were shaking their heads and scolding. No one stepped aside to let her go.

"Now you've done it," they said.

"Way too far, princess," someone leaned in and spat.

"Now she'll really kill you."

Monique straightened up, her face all twisted.

Brook believed them.

Monique bent to grab her broken bottle off the floor. It dripped in the low light.

That's my blood, Brook thought. You've got no right, no right at all.

The bigger girl grinned. "This was just for fun—but not anymore. If they ever find you, no one's even gonna recognize you. I'll take this broken glass and twist it–"

"NOO!" Brook screamed.

When Monique lunged, Brook spun on the balls of her feet and stabbed down blindly with the shork. And magic happened. Dark, horrible magic.

The broken bottle clanged off the washer.

The shork shivered in Brook's hand.

Soft as butter, even softer. The flat dent at the bottom of Monique's skull, where the shork slid down and stuck like it had hit a plate. Brook stepped back, staring.

Had she done this?

Monique dropped like a toy that had been turned off. Red was everywhere. Spraying, splashing, dripping red—and screaming, lots of screaming, but not from Monique.

Running feet. Then silence.

Everything wet and red under the bare lightbulbs.

It had been so easy. Brook hadn't even tried.

The shork fell from her shaking fingers. Her knees began to give way, but she grabbed a dryer for support and hauled herself up, away from the bloody floor. Knobs and dials dug into her back as she hugged her knees, rocking back and forth.

"I didn't mean to," she sobbed. "You should've let me go."

The shadows pressed in, red and black, and she closed her eyes against her tears. The darkness behind her eyelids was thick and gritty. The basement dripped and seeped its way inside.

Now the same darkness filled the tower as wind gusted her shoulders, whirling into the dark shaft. The dark clung to her, coated her skin and rustled against her insides. *Come on down, Brook. Lean over the edge.*

"I deserve to be here." Brook's voice was choked. "Because of what I did. And I guess I knew it the whole time, I just didn't want to..." She couldn't continue. So she inched her toes over the balcony. The bottom was so far down she couldn't see it. Maybe there was no bottom at all, and she'd keep falling and falling until she fell asleep.

She leaned into the drafty dark. *That's right*, the island said. Then something caught her eye and froze her at the edge, knees bent, hands half covering her face.

Gold coins glowed in the shadows. Floating in the dark. Yellow and round, shining like a king had tossed them to a happy crowd of kids, and the wealth had paused to flash and shimmer in midair. The flock of golden coins hovered, waiting to swerve and dart away.

Magic.

Brook drew a long breath. She waited for the gold to rise into the sky and become part of a far-off sunrise. To leave her in the dark. But the magic stayed.

"Oh, thank you," she whispered.

Then she realized the coins were leaves—golden leaves on a stubborn, dark-defying vine. They were even better than coins because they were alive. She let out a sigh.

"You're beautiful," she said. "You're something that shouldn't be here. You're something good in a horrible, horrible place. And you're here"—she gasped—"for me."

The magic glowed softly in the shadows.

Brook stood up straight in the hungry silence.

"No," she told the island. "No, I won't. I'm not alone, and I can be someone different. There's magic helping me, so I know"—she shuddered—"things can change." Her whole body shook as she stepped back from the edge and the wind died with an angry *whuff*.

Then her stomach bent in on itself and crashed up and down like the ocean under the cliffs. She put her hands against the wall and puked off the edge. When she could breathe again, she felt another shadow at her elbow—but this one was human.

Fox stood behind her in the doorway.

Brook brushed at her eyes, flicking tears away, but they overflowed down her face and chin. "Fox, they ruined the castle," she said. "They trashed it and I couldn't find the key."

Death Dogs howled somewhere far below.

"I'm sorry, Brook." Fox sounded angry. "They're a bunch of cheaters."

"Maybe we could fix it…"

"Of course we can. We can still be king and queen—it'll just mean a lot of work."

Brook wiped her face and picked up Isabella. "What about the key?"

"Knowing the blue-faces–"

"They probably threw it away."

"Yeah. C'mon, Brook. Let's get out of here."

He turned to go and she followed him without question. The cold, dark stairs went on forever. How she'd climbed them so fast, she'd never know. When they crossed landings, she heard noises down side passages. A rasp of metal, footfalls, a muffled cough: The blue-faces were waking up. She was surprised they weren't moving faster.

She and Fox moved faster, though.

"Why are we going down?" she whispered.

"I was in a rush to find you," Fox said. "Now I've got to be sure about that door."

She nodded. *See, he cares.*

At the bottom Fox checked the locks, tugging on chains,

moving bars right and left. "Hey, keep your eyes on the stairs," he said. "Stay on the lookout."

Brook turned to watch the stairway. "Do you think they'll all attack at once?"

"It's what I would expect," he said. "We have to do this exactly right."

"For sure. Hey, Foxy." She swallowed. "Thanks for coming to find me. I felt—all alone."

Fox stopped fiddling with the door. "Of course, Brook. Always."

And as awful as the night was, Brook felt better. The castle was horrible but they could improve it. Something good could happen. And she wasn't by herself. She felt warm, even though the blue-faces were on the hunt and she was shut in by tons of stone.

She was about to tell Fox that maybe, just maybe, they had a chance, and that he could rely on her more than he thought. With her eyes still on the stairs, she said, "Hey, Fox"—when cold air hit her back. Wind rushed across the landing with a groan of hinges.

Brook spun around. "Oh no!"

The castle door stood open.

She stared. "Fox, what happened?"

They looked out side by side.

She took a step forward. "Let's get this closed before–"

"Sorry, Brook." She felt his hand on her arm, squeezing tight. "I really am." Then he shoved her through the doorway and out into the night.

DEATH DOGS

Brook screamed as she fell down the stairs. She landed with a jolt, scraping her hands and knees as Isabella clattered on the stones. When she looked up, Fox stood in the doorway. For a few long moments, she didn't move. She couldn't. Her heart ached like she'd been stabbed and she felt hot tears brimming in her eyes *again*.

How could he have done that?

Was it supposed to be a joke?

She was about to run at Fox and hit him, hard, when she saw his face.

His grin twisted up at the corners.

Brook couldn't believe it.

"Move on down," he said. "I'll be right behind you."

"What are you doing?"

"Saving your life, so move. There's not a lot of room for error."

Brook picked up Isabella and squeezed her weapon tight. The weight of the night pressed down on her, and she thought she might sink into the ground. She felt like something incredibly valuable, a treasure, had been grabbed right out of her arms.

"It's you, isn't it," she said. "Not the blue-faces. It's you."

She'd never seen him look so happy.

Something tight and controlled inside him had got out.

Over her shoulder, green flames flashed close and sped away, then flashed close again.

The Death Dogs.

"You really ticked me off, you know," Fox said. "When you ran up the stairs. It could've ruined everything, but I like you, Brook, always have. So I came in after you, and luckily, like a good girl, you followed me right back out. And those gutless blues didn't attack us when they had the chance, and my dogs are still waiting. So—SO—the game is still on!"

The energy crackling from his eyes was crazy. "Here's how this will work, Brook. The dogs will empty the whole castle like a cleaning crew and I'll stroll in to pick up the pieces—and then I'll win. I'll be in charge! And I couldn't have done it without you. So thank you, Brook, I owe you. You're the secret sauce— you're the MVP. They would never, ever, in a million years, have opened that door for me."

So many things were rushing through her mind. She saw Fox finding her in the sand. Showing her the secret camp. Eating rabbit across the fire. Hiking with her through the woods. All that time acting as if he liked her—all of it leading to this.

It was too much. She couldn't make it work. Even now, after he'd thrown her down the stairs, she wanted to say, You're kidding, right Fox? We're still a team? But he wasn't kidding. They weren't a team. Nothing was like he'd said. The castle, their plan, the key. All of it, gone. And Fox was gone too. This Fox, grinning at her, she didn't know.

"You're a liar," she said. "All you do is lie, lie, lie. And we could've won together."

He shook his head no, looking smug and sad at the same time.

"Well, you're not throwing me away," Brook said. "You're losing me. I'm leaving." She leaned her scythe-staff gently against the wall and picked up the nasty-looking trident instead.

"You shouldn't have—what's the word?—leaned on me," Fox said. "You shouldn't have acted like I'd really carry your weight. Friends don't exist in real life, Brook. I think deep down, we both know that."

She held the handle of the trident to her forehead and gave herself five seconds, closing her eyes. This is the real Fox, she thought, the one you thought might be there and hoped was not. He tricked you—so no more hiding. Nothing to hold back now.

She leaned against the castle as hungry shadows gathered, circling and snapping under the moon. The massive stones felt like the safe walls of their secret campsite—another lie.

Even if you're surrounded by lies, you can still be you. So hush. Stay in charge. Do what you can. She thought about the open castle door and the terrified kids inside. And a safe, quiet room in a tower that didn't exist.

She stepped away from the stairs and into the cold, dark night.

The shapes of the Death Dogs stalked closer, jagged and bristling.

"Step aside," Fox said. "You don't need to get hurt. I'll handle them, and you can use that speed of yours and run away. You were great, Brook. You served your purpose. But now your part is over, so step off. Take a timeout or something."

"Don't tell me what to do," Brook said.

Fox glided down the stairs. At the bottom, he paused dramatically. "You know who the dogs are tracking, right? It's not me. It's you."

She stared at him. Her hand flew to her face, sticky with rabbit blood.

He'd pretended it was no big deal, like putting on make-up.

He'd made her the bait.

He'd lied. He'd liedliedlied.

Fox lifted his feet, tugging off his shoes. "I gave the dogs a little help," he admitted. "Stomped in rabbit guts, not that I needed to, and now we have that poor kid, bleeding all over inside. Death Dogs are basically land sharks, you know. Working themselves into a feeding frenzy. So get outta the way. Everything's falling into place."

She didn't move.

"Seriously, Brook, if I were you, I'd run—not now, not out there with the Death Dogs—but once they're inside, headed up the stairs, you'll have a chance. They'll be busy for a while. You can have the old campsite, I don't mind."

Until you come to take those weapons, she thought. Then you'll mind. You just want me out of the way now, so I don't confuse your pack of monsters.

Her whole body felt like fire.

Fox frowned. "Don't be stubborn, Brook."

She forced herself to look at the Death Dogs.

Eyes glowing, teeth snapping, they looked like hyenas on the nature channel. But they kept getting bigger, bigger than Rottweilers or Pit Bulls, bigger than the biggest dogs she'd ever seen. Saliva dripped from their teeth and Fox hadn't lied about their stingers. The gray-black fur gave way to barbs that swayed and jabbed like scorpion tails.

One of them lunged at her and she jerked away. Two more of them crept closer on her right and left. She couldn't fight them all. She couldn't stop them. So she did what Fox wanted. Stepped away from the stairs, out of the way.

"Good girl," Fox said. He rubbed his shoes together, still dripping rabbit blood, and the Death Dogs strained toward him, snarling. He tossed the shoes inside the castle. "Door's open, boys."

The first dog shot past in a spiny blur, claws scrabbling on the stone. When it reached the pool of the boy's blood, it tilted its long snout to the sky and howled. The other dogs rushed forward, parting around Fox like he was made of stone. A fight broke out on the stairs, dogs snarling and biting to get inside. More of them kept coming, pouring out of the dark like bats —*like bats out of the night*. Brook drew a quick, wet breath.

"It's like I'm one of them," Fox whispered, more focused on the dogs than her.

Hearing him talk like that helped.

And he didn't notice the Death Dogs parted around her too. They gave her space, even though her face and hip were streaked with blood. Even though they'd been tracking her over the plains. They wanted no part of her now that she was ready for a fight. Maybe they could smell her anger. Maybe they could smell her heart. She moved Snake-Tooth higher in her pocket. Hopefully he was on her side now that he'd got what he wanted.

"Now's the time," Fox said. "Aren't you going to run? I pulled you out of the castle on purpose, Brook. I'm giving you a chance. You earned it."

Brook shook her head. She noticed he'd picked up the spear from the bottom of the stairs. He had the axe over his shoulder, no big deal, like a baseball bat.

"I wish you would," Fox said. "I don't want to see them catch you. I like the idea of you being out there, Brook. Can't you see that?"

She wrapped her fingers around the trident.

Deadly and three-tined and razor-sharp. A familiar, hungry shape.

Welcome back, shork, she thought.

"Monsters don't always get what they want," she said.

WHO WE REALLY ARE

When she leveled the trident at Fox, it gleamed silvery-blue in the moonlight.

She flipped the switch in her head.

"Drop your weapons," she said.

Fox laughed. "Brook, c'mon. It's cute, but you really, really don't want to do this."

Brook slashed at him, a diagonal stroke from left to right, and he snapped his mouth shut and jumped back. She tried a straight jab, and he brought the axe down awkwardly to stop her, but one of the tines scraped a red line on his shin. She saw a question flicker in his eyes, and rocked another jab in hard and fast, the way you did when a bully gave you an opening.

The reach and speed of the trident took her breath away. It was as deadly as a hundred shorks. Fox swung the spear upright across his body, catching her next jab, but her blow tore the spear away and spun it into the grass. Brook snatched her weapon back and leveled it again.

"Magic brought me here," she said. "Good magic—and it's on my side. But don't worry. You still have the axe."

Now he was angry, and Brook took a deep breath and

196

braced herself. Ants crawled up her spine, rustling over the nape of her neck and turning to march back down. Up and down, up and down, dozens of ants with tiny, icy legs.

Fox stalked forward. "Who are you, Brook?" He swung the axe, a flashing arc, trying to smash the trident from her hands.

She stepped aside and made him jump back with a twisting jab. Letting loose all the quickness, all the rhythm, she'd done her best to bury since she'd arrived. She wasn't defenseless. She wasn't clueless. She was deadly. Now he'd find out.

"I thought I knew you," Fox said.

"And I thought I knew you," she said. "We were both wrong I guess."

The axe and trident met head-on with a grating crash that threw off sparks. It's an awkward match-up, Brook thought. Fox could've pinned me to the wall if he'd kept the spear. Instead, we both have to be cautious. The trident was quick—the axe was crushing. But she didn't think his cautiousness would last.

"Who taught you?" he snarled. "Where are you really from?"

"Try living in an orphanage for years," Brook snapped. "With people who hate you and who you hate back."

"I don't believe you." Fox chopped down at her, pivoted when she darted away, and swung the axe crosswise at her chest. The blow could've crushed a car door but she saw it coming and ducked. She snaked the trident out as the axe's breeze fanned her hair, and Fox jumped back like he'd been stung.

"Good job, shork," Brook whispered.

Fox spat into the grass. "They sent you, didn't they? To get close to me and take me out—that's even more twisted than the dragon." He didn't seem to care that one of his knees was bleeding.

"They?" Brook said. "Who's 'they?' Don't be an idiot. And don't pretend you trusted me—you didn't even like me!" Anger raced along her veins, melting all the ants. She cocked her right elbow and drove the trident forward, once, twice, three times. The axe wasn't made for defense. Fox knocked the first blow aside, dodged the second—then his upper arm was bleeding.

"Where—are—we?" she said through her teeth.

His eyes were shadows. Then he grinned. "You'd have to kill me before I told you, Brook. But that won't happen." He dropped the axe and her eyes widened. Fox snatched at his clothing, and she had the strange thought that he was on fire, trying to put himself out. Instead, something silver shot through the air.

Brook threw herself aside, but the knife still got her, ripping her t-shirt, slicing her shoulder, hitting the castle wall.

"I don't want to kill you, Brook—and I'm not lying when I say that." Now Fox was holding the spear. He'd marked its place in the grass. "Tell me all about yourself."

She bit the side of her cheek. Blood trickled from her shoulder. Inside the castle, someone screamed. How long had they been fighting? Just minutes that seemed like seconds that seemed like hours. And now the fight was almost over.

"Who are those kids?" she said. "The blue-faces."

Fox blinked. "Scared little brats, not a single one of them really dangerous. Not a single one of them highly rated. Keeping me out of my own castle, can you believe it? Locked outside, with all the ferals trying to hunt me down. But now I'm back in charge, and it's your turn, Brook. Who are you and why are you really here?"

LAST DANCE

BROOK THOUGHT ABOUT MAKING SOMETHING UP.

"I was sent here to spy on you, Fox," she could say. Even better, "I was sent here to sabotage you..." Something to keep him guessing, because she didn't see how she could stop the blood flowing from her shoulder while she held onto the new shork. If she kept bleeding, the pain would fade, and she'd get numb, and she'd take three steps to the castle and lean against the wall, or maybe sit on the stairs until she fell over.

Or maybe Fox would kill her first.

But she didn't have the heart to make something up. And who was supposed to have sent her? The dragon? The Foundation? Fox's parents, furious their baby wasn't dead? No, nothing made any sense.

"I'm supposed to be here," she said. "I deserve it. I killed a girl in the Foundation basement, so that's what it must be. Even though I thought—I thought..."

I thought there was magic. And I thought it could help me be a hero, and that it was waiting for me, waiting to make something good happen in a horrible place. But I'm so stupid. I was wrong.

Fox narrowed his eyes. "I don't get it," he said. "I don't see your play."

There were howls and shouts and crashing in the castle now. Behind the massive walls, raised voices sounded tinny and far away. Brook pictured Death Dogs racing down halls, bounding up stairs, hunting the blue-faces from room to room. She hoped the kids were organized, that they'd woken up fast and hadn't been surprised by hungry eyes staring down at them.

"I don't have a play." Brook took a hand off the trident and pressed her bleeding shoulder and she knew it was the truth. "That's who I am, just someone no one wanted, who decided to fight back. Otherwise, I'd be dead. Since I'm not dead, I'm here. That's the whole story." Anger rose in her again, but she could feel it seeping away like water as soon as it reached her heart.

"Oh." Fox passed a hand over his eyes. "That's all?" He sighed. "If that's really who you are, Brook, you have nothing to be ashamed of. Whoever you killed, she deserved it." He frowned. "I wasn't lying before, when you found all my weapons. I'm an orphan, too. I may have already said this—I lose track—but I was never wanted. They wanted to wipe me off the earth. Delete me, and they'd never even seen me, can you believe that? There's a word for it that I can't remember..."

Brook slid a little down the wall.

Fox trailed a finger under his eyes. "And you know what else? Half the time I wish they'd gotten away with it. Because then I wouldn't be here, would I? And I wouldn't feel so—rageful all the time." He cleared his throat. "I also didn't lie when I said I liked you, Brook. You're smart and a helluva better fighter than I thought. But I have to beat this island—burn it, break it, smash it—I have to win." A shadow moved over his face. "I can't let you ruin this. Not when I've waited so long."

He raised the spear.

Brook held her bloody hand against her shoulder. She wasn't sure what she could've ruined, what she could've possibly taken from Fox. He did whatever he wanted. She'd tried to stop him and failed.

"For once I wish I didn't have to do this," Fox said.

"Then don't." Brook felt darkness growing in her head. Blood ran down her elbow, making her feel cold. "You already won," she said. "You got what you wanted. No one can beat you, everyone's afraid of you—you got the castle. What if you never have to worry about me? I won't sneak up on you. I won't try to get you when you're not looking…"

She found herself sitting on the ground. Now there was black space behind her eyes, making her say things she wouldn't normally say. "We could be the king and queen, like we joked about, and we could change things. Fox, *we* could change. We could kill the Death Dogs and leave the other kids alone, at least the scared ones. Things could be different. We could become different people, like the good kids in the *Lord of the Flies*…"

She realized she was going on and on, and she was slipping sideways, grass brushing her face. She grabbed the trident to stay upright. Fox's shape was blurry against the brightening sky, and she squinted to bring him into focus. She had the idea he'd been listening, even leaning toward her. His spear was still raised, but resting on a bony shoulder. His other hand was touching his forehead. His eyes looked like the ashes of the fire in their secret campsite. When he finally spoke, his voice caught, like her hair in the thorns all those days ago.

"I can't, Brook. I wish I could do that but I can't. I don't think you can either. We'd be making promises we can't keep, and it would make us weak, and someone else would take advantage, and then—they'd all close in. They won't let us change like that. That's not how the island works. Not how anything works." He drew his knuckles across his eyes and when his hand came down, he looked fierce. "Anyway, I don't want to change."

Dawn glimmered on the long blade of the spear. Brook tried to lift the trident but she couldn't. Her arms felt like straws. She let them drop to her knees and the new shork fell against her shoulder. Her bloody fingers touched Snake-Tooth's handle. She forced herself to look at Fox as she tugged the knife from her pocket.

"Don't do that." He shook his head. "Don't."

She felt the familiar hilt in her palm, but she couldn't hold on. The knife slipped through her fingers and fell in the grass.

His spear blade hovered inches from her throat.

"Sorry, Brook," Fox said. "You're a good person."

She closed her eyes and turned away. She could've sworn he meant it.

Something like ice brushed her neck. She was so tired. Maybe it wouldn't be so bad.

God, I'm sorry, she thought. I wanted to be someone else.

DRAGON

THE SKY WENT DARK. THERE WAS A ROAR AND A FLASH OF HEAT. Brook lost all sense of where she was. She had the feeling Fox had been suddenly snatched away, or she'd been grabbed away from him.

This is hell, she thought. This is death. And she wondered how much worse it got. There was no pressure at her neck. If her throat was cut, she couldn't tell, because it seemed like she was still breathing. A rough, cold surface pushed against her back, but the rest of her felt numb and floaty. There was pain but not too awful.

Someone was shouting and coming closer, more than one someone. There was a yell, metal scraping metal. Brook pictured angry devils, herding people with pitchforks. Oh no. Her mouth felt dry. *Devils carry shorks!* How had she never seen it?

She shuddered. Now it was too late. She was definitely in hell, and the bad part was about to start. With her eyes squeezed shut, she thought, Maybe if I hold very still, they'll leave me until later. Maybe they'll take me last.

But she knew they wouldn't, so she finally opened her eyes.

She saw the dragon.

Crouched on the edge of the eastern plain, wings folded, neck snaked low, the sunrise shimmered at the edges of its huge body. Even from where she slumped against the castle, Brook felt heat rising off the beast in waves. Human shapes were running past like they were racing—the ones she'd thought were devils—sprinting by, one after another, light gleaming off helmets and boots—and guns? They disappeared into the castle. Were these people on Fox's side?

But Fox didn't have anyone. That's why he was the way he was.

Brook's chest tightened as she scrabbled upright, catching herself on the stones. Her feet were like slippery bars of soap. She fell against the castle, pressed a hand to her shoulder and blinked. Could this be a rescue? Or were the soldiers running from the dragon? Nothing made sense.

She tried to focus her blurry vision. The dragon was in no hurry. Its blue-black scales glittered as it watched her, swaying in the yellow dawn. From time to time it hissed. Taking her in. Deciding what to do.

Because the dragon had to be in charge. It had sent the fighters in. Now it was making up its fierce and hungry mind, thinking, What should I do with this tiny girl? Brook knew she smelled like blood and exhaustion and death, which was bad. But maybe dragons weren't like Death Dogs. Maybe they liked a challenge.

Who knew what dragons liked?

Then the dragon twisted, and she flattened her palms against the stone—but it didn't lunge at her. Instead, it shifted its weight lazily, scales creaking with a *whush* of escaping smoke. Another shape moved toward her, stepping off the dragon's bent hind leg. Had he been riding on its back?

Someone big and dark stood over her. With the rising sun behind him, it was hard to see anything about him except that he was tall. She hunched against the wall, waiting to see what he would do.

"You were impressive," the man said. "We didn't see it coming, didn't think you'd stand a chance. He's lethal, the top dog, and we've known it for a while, but you're a close second. Or you were. Not much of a threat now are you?" He leaned in closer.

Brook made out dark eyes, a face used to being in charge.

She held as still as she could.

"You need medical attention," the man said. "You're worse than I thought."

"Is this...a rescue?" Brook whispered.

"Absolutely, sweetheart," the man said. "You've got all kinds of potential, and our favorite troublemaker had you hidden away. Of course we saw you—tried to scoop you up in the woods—but we had no idea what you could do. He tried to save you for himself, which is just like him. So much like him, I want to shake him until his teeth rattle. Maybe I will." He stood up. "I'm going to move you now."

"Oh, no, don't." Brook didn't like the sound of that. She was feeling more sleepy every second, and she didn't want to be touched, not by anyone. But maybe just this once, since it was a rescue...

"Try to relax." The man paused. "On second thought, you're relaxed enough. Try to stay awake. And no stabbing me with hidden weapons, that will go badly. I'm on your side."

Brook felt his fingers, hard and strong, slip behind her back. His other arm swept up her knees. As he lifted her easily, she tried not to flop. They stood by the back door of the castle as the man glared inside. Brook wondered what they were waiting for. She took the moment to look up at his face. Fierce eyes, a strong jaw, a calculating look on his face. This was someone you didn't want to cross.

The man shrugged, and Brook rose and fell with the movement of his shoulders. His clothing rustled in a stiff, plastic-like way. "Let's hope it's going well in there. Talk about a tactical nightmare. The whole island needs to be reset, picked up and shaken, everyone put on notice. We won't stand by and watch the population get liquidated. But you're my priority now. What do you call yourself?"

Nothing the man said had made her think their conversation was going to be two-sided, so Brook took a moment to think.

"Brook," she half-whispered.

He nodded down at her. "Ok Brook, don't be scared." He swiveled away from the shadows, and sunlight blinded her. She felt the man's footsteps, long and steady, crunching through the field, moving through the grass.

Brook twisted in his arms, but he was too strong.

She wanted to scream.

He was taking her to the dragon.

BELLY OF THE BEAST

BROOK HAD EXPECTED TO BE DEAD ALREADY, SLUMPED SIDEWAYS against the castle wall. Now she suddenly knew the soldier—that's what he seemed to be—would shovel her into the dragon's mouth. This wasn't a rescue. He wasn't the rescuing type.

The soldier barely noticed she was struggling. As weak as she was, it probably felt like he was carrying a toddler. "Shush, shush," he said, tightening his grip. "You've come so far. Don't lose your head now."

She half-closed her eyes as they came even with the dragon's huge, triangular snout. Smoke rose from nostrils dark as gun barrels. Hungry yellow eyes watched them, flat and wicked like tinted glass. She was grateful its jaws were shut. The edges of its teeth gleamed like the wide ends of knives.

The soldier elbowed the dragon's monstrous head. Brook bit her lip to keep from screaming as its mouth gaped wider.

The soldier winked at her and snorted. "Stand down, beast," he told the dragon.

Brook tried to hold still as they walked past.

"I thought about snatching you from the air," the man said. "But things were complicated. Death Dogs on the hunt, kids running through the castle, your friend turning everything to hash. I think if we'd flown over and tried to pick you up, we might've just shredded you. Honestly, you look half-shredded already. I feel like I'm carrying hollow bones." He gave her a toss.

"Oww," Brook said.

Maybe he didn't know how strong he was. Or maybe he was showing off.

The soldier's feet creaked on the dragon's armored leg, which bent at a right angle, claws sunk in the turf. The soldier kicked the dragon's ribs, making it twitch and hiss, and Brook jerked in his arms. A door slid open in the monster's ribcage.

They stepped inside.

All the air drained from Brook's lungs and the blood ran away from her face. The beast's belly looked like the interior of a plane, the kind you saw in hero movies. Metal benches with grips and harnesses lined the walls. Rows of weapons rested in brackets. Lights glowed in a metal ceiling.

The soldier was watching her face. He let out a laugh. "Priceless. Absolutely priceless. If my hands were free, I'd snap a picture. You see, you've got nothing to worry about. Let's get you to the medical room."

Brook's brain couldn't keep up. She kept expecting to see light glowing redly through the walls, shining through dragon skin and arteries, revealing a huge reptilian skeleton. But all she saw were sleek, modern rooms with curving walls. It made her stomach twist and her brain thud against the sides of her skull. Every few steps, the man glanced down at her and smiled.

"I know," he said. "I know. And he didn't tell you. Of course he didn't, just like him."

When he set her on a long, white table, Brook's eyelids were fluttering. She couldn't seem to make them stop.

"Stay with me," the soldier said. "You're valuable—what's your name—Brook? You're valuable, Brook. I don't want to lose you. Don't get me wrong, everyone has *some* value—everyone who survives, obviously, everyone who makes it—but you're special. Let's start with an IV." She felt the needle prick her arm. "Give this a minute, then it's stitches. Nice thing about knife wounds, good clean edges. Easy to tie back together. A to B, B to A, like shoelaces. Nothing nasty for me to dig out inside."

He's honest, Brook thought. Not like Fox. But his honesty is not very nice.

When she felt the next needle bite into her shoulder, she gulped a deep breath, trying to stay awake, to keep an eye on the soldier. She couldn't help thinking about him digging around, cutting shreds of evil out. It was a horrible thought. He'd have to cut her open with a scalpel, wearing scrubs and a mask like in the ER shows.

Her chest would be folded open, flooded with white light as he carved at all the shards of darkness in her heart. What would be left of her when he was done? A pile of bones? She felt her fingers twitching. She bit her tongue and tasted blood.

"Noo," she groaned.

"Take it easy," the man said.

His needle poked her shoulder again.

She blacked out.

THE FIRST OF MANY SECRETS

BROOK STARED AT THE RIBBED SILVER CEILING AND TRIED TO match it to a place she knew. The bright, clean lines were new and expensive. A hooded lamp bent over her like it was worried about her health.

This wasn't Weed Middle School, with its dirty lockers and fluorescent lighting. It wasn't the Children's Foundation. The nurse there only gave out aspirin. Brook twitched a hand up from the table and put it on her stomach.

Instantly, her shoulder flared with pain. Her hip ached. Her head throbbed.

She wished she hadn't moved at all.

She wished it even more as she remembered she was on an island, and she'd had one friend but he had tried to kill her. The dragon had come down from the sky but it wasn't real. And that's where she was, inside the dragon. This bright, clean place where there was hardly room to move.

She wanted to get out and run across the plains and plunge into the forest. She'd give the Death Dogs the slip and build a fire in some hidden spot where she could fall asleep after a bath in the creek. But she knew those things would never happen.

The soldier wouldn't let her. The soldier—no, the commander, and his team of soldiers—they were the ones in charge. The dragon was a lie, just like the castle was a lie, and Fox. The whole island was a maze of lies that would kill you just as quickly as the truth.

Her body felt heavy. The hospital table pushed hard against her spine.

Brook knew she deserved to be there. She'd taken her shork and stuck it into Monique's brainstem and now, remembering it clearly, she couldn't allow herself to mind. Not one bit. Look at where caring had got her. If she cared, she might as well give up. She might as well be dead. No, she couldn't mind.

I don't mind, she told herself. I don't, I don't.

Brook sat up carefully and swung her legs over the side. Her heart was pounding hot and heavy like a monster trying to get out, because even though she knew this was her fault, there was nothing she could do about the way she felt. Her heart was like the fire in their ruined campsite, coals glowing under ash. Banked down, waiting for the moment it would roar to life. So angry. So, so angry.

She clenched her fists and pushed herself off the table. She was still wearing her bloody, tattered t-shirt, cut away at one shoulder, but there was a clean shirt folded on a chair. She pulled off the rags of her old shirt and threw them in a sterile-looking trash can.

The stitches in her shoulder were neat and dark like a lightning bolt with lots of zigs and zags. Her skin had closed right up. But the flesh below kept aching. She shrugged the clean black shirt over her head, wincing when she lifted her arm. It fit her snugly. The fabric was thick and stretchy, better than anything she'd ever owned.

No one seemed to be keeping an eye on her, but that was just another lie. Still, she was tired of waiting in the safe-seeming surgery. Outside the medical room, she found herself in a compact kitchen. Bright lights gleamed on chrome and white appliances. Brook stared at an industrial fridge. Her stomach ached, but she didn't want to eat. She wanted to dump food on the floor, splash it across the perfect kitchen—unless there was chocolate milk. But this was some kind of army plane, so there wouldn't be.

She moved unsteadily over the tile, lurching now and then. Her hip stung like someone was jabbing it with needles. She tugged at the waistline of her shorts and found more stitches. Of course. Snake-Tooth had bit deeper than she'd thought.

Why had she bothered naming him?

When she opened the fridge, cartons of milk lined the top shelf. Brook froze when she saw one row was chocolate. She picked up a quart, then flung her arm across the shelf and flailed. Containers smacked the polished floor. They bounced but didn't spill.

Brook wanted to scream. She waited for someone to come rushing through the door, but no one did. No one shouted at her. No one helped her make the mess she wanted. She let the fridge swing shut and moved along a table. The cold tiles seemed to tilt under her feet and she paused to catch her balance. Where were her shoes and socks?

When she shoved the next door open and stepped through, the first thing she noticed was the carpet. Soft to stand on, an expensive feel. When she looked up, she realized she'd walked into a meeting. The room was a thin lounge, lights glowing in the walls, a small table bolted to the floor. The soldier-commander sprawled across a chair. A bloody, angry-looking child sat upright in another.

The milk carton froze at Brook's lips when she realized it was Fox.

"Nice to see you're not leaking blood," the grown-up said. "Call me DaVinci. I was just making things clear to your friend here."

"Hi Foxy," Brook said. "I wish I could've killed you."

Fox didn't move or answer.

DaVinci raised his eyebrows. "I feel you," he said. "We'll both need massive self-control. The island has no rules"—he jabbed a finger at Fox—"and who would've thought you could ruin anarchy? But he found a way. Everything spiraling into chaos, the ecosystem trashed, the rankings totally shot. Top prospects dropping like flies. Rising stars"—he nodded at Brook—"deceitfully hidden. Now we've got to empty the castle, bring new monsters in, reset the game."

DaVinci took a breath and clenched his fists. "Incredibly expensive, that's the point. All so we can have a proper free-for-all. This is your last chance, boy. You, on the other hand"—in a blink he was on his feet. Brook didn't have a chance to move as he wrapped a steely arm around her.

"You're in a different category, sweetheart. Your career is just beginning."

"You're lying," she said.

The man laughed and shot a look at Fox.

She thought how weird it was for Fox to be so quiet.

"Of course you think that," DaVinci said. "We've taught you well. But look around you. You've been rescued." He spread his hands. "You know the secret of the dragon—the first of many secrets. Everything's about to change. Good food, nice clothes, classes you'll be good at. If you play your cards right, you'll never see the island again."

"I don't believe you," Brook said. "Take me away from here if it's all true."

He laughed again and pushed a small white button in the wall. A section of the metal slid away, revealing tinted glass.

"Look out the window, honey."

THE DEAL

BROOK STARED DOWN AT THE OCEAN. WAVES CRASHED AS FAR AS she could see. The dark, twisting tail of the dragon lashed the breakers. There was no island. No land of any kind. Nothing but a horizon and hungry water and distant purple clouds.

Her chocolate milk hit the floor, glugging from the open carton.

DaVinci picked it up and took a sip.

"It was all pretend," Brook said, knowing that wasn't even close to what she meant.

"You're too modest," the soldier said. "Despite *his* meddling, you moved through the survival funnel. Think about it. You escaped the cliffs. You survived the clans. You even crashed the castle and gave him—what did you call him, Foxy?—a serious scare. You're fearless, darling. You're deadly. The Jabberwocky really likes you. We've moved you to the top of our draft board." He frowned and Brook wondered if there was something about the draft board he didn't like. Then she thought of all the kids Fox had killed.

"What are you asking me to do?" she said.

"To live in the real world, where the odds aren't stacked

214

against you." DaVinci's eyes burned into her. "To use your brains and your pretty face. To be the best."

"That makes no sense," she said.

DaVinci sighed. "To be a spy. There, I said it. I hate being so pedantic."

Waves lapped soundlessly outside the window.

Brook knew what it meant to be a spy. Sneaking around. Keeping an eye on everyone and giving away as little as you could. Stealing little moments for yourself. Expecting the worst and trusting no one. She'd been a spy her whole life and DaVinci was right. She was good at it. The problem was, she also hated it.

"What if I say no?" she finally said.

DaVinci smiled at her. Fox looked up and shook his head.

"I think you can probably guess," the soldier said.

"If you go back, everyone will hunt you," Fox said. "There will be a target on your back and you'll never get a chance to start a tribe or win the castle, even though you–"

"Shut up, Fox," Brook said. "I never want to hear your voice again."

DaVinci shrugged. "He knows what he's talking about, but have it your way." He held out the chocolate milk to her. "Before we continue, I need you to promise me you won't hurt Dog-Fox here."

Brook took the milk and felt her ears and face get hot. "Why would I promise that? From the moment I met him, all he's done is–"

"I won't hurt *you*," Fox said. "I thought I could, but when I tried to, I–"

"Stop!" It was more than she could take. Brook threw the milk carton at him. He ducked and it hit the wall. The attack was so weak she wanted to cry.

"Ha!" DaVinci said. "And why *would* you hurt her now that you're off the island? What could you possibly hope to gain?"

Fox shrugged. "I'm telling her so she knows–"

"STOP TALKING!" Brook yelled. *Breathe in, breathe out.* She wondered what the man would do if she ran at Fox and hit him. But she was hurt and couldn't move fast.

"There are no rules on the island," the commander said evenly. "But once we leave the island, there are rules. Rules with penalties, aren't there, Dog?"

"Yes."

"So you need to understand this, Brook."

"Ok," she said. "I get it."

"Let me just finish my speech," he said. "You're being sent to a wonderful place. In fact, and you'll love this, some people call it *magical.* How cute, how ignorant—*magic*—so you'll be able to ride unicorns and talk to the trees. More to the point, you'll have nice clothes, good food, money, education, a tolerable amount of safety. Classes you'll enjoy and be good at. Chances to win awards or play around at making friends. Who knows where this will end if you don't blow your cover?"

"Magic," Brook said. "Great. And you'll be watching."

"Of course I will." DaVinci laughed. "Just like on the island but more so. I was going to save this for later, but since you mention it"—he grinned. "I'll be going with you. Education plus espionage is my sweet spot."

Fox's shoulders gave a little jerk.

"Everything will change for you, Brook," the soldier said. "You'll be the best, with connections in two different worlds. I expect great things from you. You'll thrive in a new situation." He uncrossed his legs and stood. "You'll absolutely love it in Sylvan Woods."

DaVinci hit buttons on a keypad and a door slid open. Brook saw the dragon's cargo area full of soldiers before he stepped through and the door slid shut behind him.

She and Fox stared at each other.

Brook stepped away and stood in the kitchen door. She wasn't sure where to go.

"You liar," she said. "You nasty, dirty–" She caught herself and brushed her hair back from her face. A few strands almost touched her shoulders now. "You will never fool me again," she said. "Never. Ever, ever."

"I hope you're right, Brook." Fox looked pale but she saw a trace of his old smile. It looked like fake jewelry to her now.

"You knew all along," she said. "About the island."

"I made a mistake." Fox sat up straight. "I admit it. We could've held them off, Brook. We could've hid inside the castle. The Death Dogs could've been our guard dogs. He"—they both glanced toward the door—"*He* would've had to leave us alone or burn the castle down. It could've worked. I didn't see it until too late. I'm sorry."

"We'll never know," Brook said. "Since you tried to kill me."

"I admit, I thought about it," Fox said. "But if I'd tried, really tried—do you really think you'd be here?" He traced a red slash across his face. She couldn't tell if it was his blood or someone else's—and she didn't answer his question.

"I wanted to burn everything down," he said. "Or get off that cursed island. The whole game was rigged against me when they sent me back, and I had to mess things up, make something happen." His fingers clenched the edges of his chair. "I wanted to ruin everything. Total chaos…or escape…I would've taken either one."

"Oh, I see" she said. "Then I guess you got what you wanted."

"Yeah." But this time he didn't smile. And in a stupid way, she wished he would, because it would be easier to hate him. And because at least someone would be happy.

"It's just that I'm so angry all the time," Fox said. "In my bones."

"Let me guess," Brook said. "It comes from never being wanted."

"So I told you?" he said. "I lose track."

"I feel it too," she said. "I snap my fingers and it's there. It comes from being treated like you're nothing. A no one. A thing no one wants. It makes you wonder what's wrong with you, but there's nothing wrong with me. Nothing wrong. Nothing."

"Of course there isn't," Fox said.

And she knew he felt the same way, but she still couldn't forgive him for everything he'd done. Because no matter how you felt, you still had choices.

Fox looked at the floor.

"Are you going," she asked. "Going to Sylvan Woods?"

"Of course I'm going," he said bitterly.

After a minute, Brook sat down in the second chair and looked out the window. Endless waves crashed under them, gray-green and capped with white and full of darkness underneath.

Somewhere out there, she thought, is a room with a big door and a lock, where warm sunlight spills in puddles on the floor. And I'll stay there for as long as I like and when I'm ready I will step outside and people will see there is more to me. Down here, right here, just waiting. I can be sweet and pretty. I can be tough and take care of myself.

I can be the best, just the best.

She half-closed her eyes.

And people will wish I was their girl, she thought, but I won't be. No one will be allowed to touch me. Maybe I'll have friends but probably not, since you can't trust anyone. And even though I'm fine by myself, people will wish they knew me—when I show them I am lovable.

"There's a word for us," Fox said.

Brook opened her eyes. He was looking at the sea.

"A word for the two of us," he said, "for what we could've had, if I hadn't ruined it. It's when you know someone, really know them, and when things go badly, you know that person will come, no matter what."

Brook tapped a rhythm on the arms of her chair.

"They'll crash in and do whatever they can," Fox said, "no matter how bad things are. And you know they will, you *know* it"—he touched the side of his head—"because they've proven it, proven they're solid, that you can count on them a hundred percent." He glanced up. "There's a word for it that I forget."

Brook dared him to meet her eyes. He didn't.

She tried to think of the missing word, and for the life of her she couldn't.

When she gave up, she brushed back the chopped ends of her hair.

She counted to ten. She counted to a hundred. Then a thousand.

Fox still hadn't met her eyes.

Waves flashed under the belly of the dragon as they sped across the sea.

———

THANKS FOR READING CROOKED CASTLE.

If you're wondering what to read next, check out *Twisting Trails*, book #3 in the Casey Grimes Series. You can learn more at **ajvanderhorst.com**.

For all the inside stuff on the Casey Grimes universe—including a free story, book news, and tips on fighting monsters—sign up for *The Sylvan Spy* at **b.link/Castle**.

ACKNOWLEDGMENTS

Big thank yous to the usual suspects at Lion & Co. Press. The more books I write, the more you pitch in. You're a gritty, glittery dream team full of passion, humor and (sometimes too much) drama. It's just a matter of time until you get notorious, and until then, I'm happy I get loads of your help. Some day we'll book a haunted castle for a ~~creative retreat~~ legendary party.

Thanks, **Gwen**, for all those morning coffees and pep talks.

Thanks, **Flannery**, for the after hours drinks and monster consultations.

Thanks, **Miles**, for the undying optimism and sales projections.

Thanks, **Ezra**, for the endless re-reads and notes on forest realism.

Thanks, **Asher**, for the concept sketches and drafting sessions.

Thanks, **Aidan**, for the frequent check-ins and knowing how to make a darn good cappuccino.

Thanks, **Lindsay**, for tugging on character arcs and plot lines until everything comes together.

Each of you help me remember that whether we find ourselves in Sylvan Woods or Crooked Castle, there's more magic in the world than we can see.

ABOUT THE AUTHOR

AJ Vanderhorst lives in tornado country with his wife, kids, and a turtle with a taste for human toes. AJ especially likes hot sauce. His award-winning fantasy books for kids take place in an alternate USA where monsters stalk the suburbs. To learn more about how to survive a monster attack, visit AJ online at **ajvanderhorst.com.**

THE END

**READY TO READ A FREE STORY,
PICK A NEW T-SHIRT, OR
JOIN A SECRET MESSAGE RING?**

**HEAD OVER TO
AJVANDERHORST.COM**